5/15

Giving Up

Mike Steeves

BOOKTHUG
DEPARTMENT OF NARRATIVE STUDIES
TORONTO, 2015

FIRST EDITION

The production of this book was made possible through the generous assistance of the Canada Council for the Arts and the Ontario Arts Council.

LIBRARY AND ARCHIVES CANADA CATALOGUING IN PUBLICATION

Steeves, Mike, 1978-, author
    Giving up / Mike Steeves.

Issued in print and electronic formats.
ISBN 978-1-77166-091-4 (pbk.).--ISBN 978-1-77166-109-6 (html)

    I. Title.

PS8637.T432G58 2015   C813'.6   C2015-900802-6
                                      C2015-900803-4

A **bundled** eBook edition is available
with the purchase of this print book.

PRINTED IN CANADA

CLEARLY PRINT YOUR NAME ABOVE IN UPPER CASE
Instructions to claim your eBook edition:
1. Download the BitLit app for Android or iOS
2. Write your name in **UPPER CASE** above
3. Use the BitLit app to submit a photo
4. Download your eBook to any device

For Nikki

*. . . the sorry and ludicrous fact with most people is, alas,
that in their own house they prefer to live in the basement.*
—Søren Kierkegaard

JAMES

The world is full of uplifting stories about extraordinary men and women who toiled away in obscurity for years and years, if not for their entire lives, before they were finally recognized, in some cases only in their afterlife, for achieving something great where so many others have failed. We constantly hear of how they stuck to their guns and defied all the odds when everyone was telling them to quit. It's rare to go a full day without nodding along to an inspiring anecdote about someone who was able to shut out all those voices telling them that they weren't good enough and that they were on the wrong path, so all they could hear was the little voice inside their head that told them they were destined for glory and that all they had to do was to stay the course. We might be sitting on a bus next to a couple of potheads, or in the lineup at a food court behind a gang of computer nerds, or maybe we bump into an old friend from high school, whatever the case is, we're forced to listen to these people talk about *a complete nobody* who endured the pity and ridicule of their entire community, until later in life he or she revealed his or her true genius and, one assumes, experienced the sort of vindication that most of us don't even dare dream of. Considering how ubiquitous these stories are, you would think that we place a high value on unwavering strength and conviction, you would think that we admire people who keep trying despite countless punishing failures, but the truth is that we only admire these people in retrospect. If we actually come across one of these singular and heroic individuals who defy all criticism, who ignore their countless defeats, who carry on despite all the evidence that they should give up, then we are invariably disgusted by what we see. We think we can tell the difference between someone who has yet to succeed versus someone who is doomed to failure, but we can't. It's impossible to tell them apart, they both come off as desperate and slightly crazed, so we get it all wrong, or try to play it safe, by rejecting the true genius and celebrating the mediocre, the sure thing. We never discover these geniuses for ourselves, it's always from someone else, which is why it takes years before we can finally recognize their accomplishments, and why many of these geniuses end up dying before word gets around. Whenever I hear about one of these great men or women who died before they could be recognized, I always wonder if they knew they were right and that everyone else was wrong. Had they discovered some sort of sign or evidence that proved, if only to themselves, that their destiny would be fulfilled? I'm particularly curious because I decided at a very young age that I was going to devote my life to accomplishing something extraordinary, but now I'm worried that I've made a huge mistake. Maybe I should give up. Maybe it's insane to keep going when everything I've done up to this point clearly indicates that there's no greatness in store for me. I've been concerned about this for a while now. I worry out loud to anyone who will listen, but this is all just for show, and doesn't affect my conviction. If anything, it strengthens my resolve. If I gave up now then I would be admitting that my entire life had been a waste, or, if not a complete waste, then it was the equivalent of walking in the wrong direction for twenty years, and, losing all hope of ever finding my way back, laying down on the ground where I stood and waiting for sleep, or whatever, to come over me. There didn't seem to be any use in turning around at this point, so just like all the countless other failures out there, I'm trapped by my own unyielding determination. The supreme irony of it is that even though I am wasting my time I feel as though I'm superior to all those who, rather than devote themselves to achieving the impossible, spend their lives accomplishing easily defined and reachable goals. And it's feelings like these that have led me to think that maybe it's time to give up. Maybe giving up on these pretensions is the more courageous thing to do. Even though we never tell stories about the people who took the advice of their family and friends – especially because we don't tell stories about these advice-takers – it no doubt takes way more guts to admit that the course you have been following, that you have shaped every aspect of your life around, was precisely the wrong course to take. (This was the big lesson from my encounter with the con man.) And there is an additional moral imperative for giving up, of course, since I'm not the only one heading in the wrong direction – I'm dragging my wife along with me. Every day, she puts her faith in me and trusts that I'm leading her in the right direction, that the course that I have chosen for myself will inadvertently also lead to the fulfillment of some of her own hopes and desires, when in fact I am leading her into total ruin. Of course the reason that she is so compliant, so willing to be led down the garden path, so to speak, is because I look her right in the eye every day and say to her, 'I know where I'm going.' Obviously she is very suspicious that I've been lying to her face. She's flat out accused me on numerous occasions. For instance, 'You have no fucking idea what you're doing,' is something she just said to me during the fight we had earlier today, before I went out and met the con man. 'I am so angry with myself for going along with this,' she said, referring to my work in the basement. 'I should have known what I was getting into.' But there was no way she could've known. When she first met me I was like everyone else my age. Back then it would've been impossible to say who was going to succeed and who was going to fail. The odds looked even. The differences that would emerge later on and set us apart so drastically weren't apparent. It's hard to believe that a true genius ever had equals or rivals for the same great goals and grand pursuits. We are convinced that they were fated to become the singular geniuses that we know them as, and it's strange to us that this may not have been obvious to everyone since the day they were born, but since we don't know what genius looks like, we can't even describe what genius *is*, and at that early age what may seem like idiocy can turn out to be a talent for concentration. So back when I was young, while you might have been able to identify a few of the more likely successes or failures, most of us were simply too insubstantial for there to be anything to base one's judgment upon. We might have been very promising, or at least not unpromising. There wouldn't have been much cause to suspect that we would end up as tragic failures, bringing our wives and our children to the brink of ruin, just as it would have been ridiculous to assume that any of us would have a great success, and become the subject of tedious anecdotes about the virtues of singular vision and perseverance. I should probably mention that Mary and I are only on the brink of ruin, and that I haven't led her so far down that we'll never find our way back up again, which is to say that there is still time for her to do a one-eighty, to refuse to be led by me any longer and go her own way, but it isn't likely that she will do this, for the same reason that I'm not going to give up at this point (which was also the reason why I didn't walk away from the con man once I knew he was full of shit). She has invested too much to pull out now, especially when there is still a remote possibility that I am actually on the right path and that success is right around the corner. What if, right after she finally gave up on me and tried to start a new life for herself, I turned out to be right all along, and the long, hard years were redeemed by recognition and success? How would she be able to live with herself knowing that if she had stayed with me for a little while longer it all would have been worth it? No, she's too invested to consider leaving, at least not for a little while longer, although there are signs that my time is running out. She's become increasingly encouraging, offering advice and assistance, which may sound like a good thing but is actually what she does when she's losing her patience. I wasn't nearly as concerned about the status of our relationship when she was openly contemptuous of how I spent my time down in the basement pursuing something that in all likelihood I was never going to achieve. Back then she wasn't worried that I was going to sabotage our lives together, she was only annoyed by how much time I was wasting down there. When she did allow a shadow of a doubt to cross her mind it was because she was worried that maybe it wasn't healthy to be so obsessed with my life's work. But she still had faith in me. When she occasionally lost her composure and accused me of using my basement-time as *an excuse for not having a life*, when she tried to start a fight by belittling the calling that I have devoted my life to, I rarely got upset because I knew that ultimately she wasn't worried about how everything was going to turn out, she just wanted me to hurry up and get things over with. I can tell that she's becoming increasingly worried because these days she is clearly making a *concerted effort* to stay positive. No more jokes about how she should've married someone else instead. 'You know,' she would say, 'someone normal?' Gone are the little tantrums she used to throw when she couldn't 'take it anymore,' after she'd come home from doing groceries to find me down in the basement while the rest of the apartment 'looked like a fucking disaster.' In its place was a sort of forced serenity, and now, instead of losing her temper, she would speak to me in a perfectly even, almost emotionless tone, and no matter what I did, despite the relentless parade of rejection and bad news I greeted her with every day, she maintained the same implacable demeanour. This shift from her prior state of annoyance and mild irritation, which only manifested itself as anger if I neglected my household duties, to her new blandly cheerful and supportive role obviously makes me suspicious and insecure, because it's clear that she's losing her faith. When I started out on this course I never imagined that I wouldn't have time to accomplish my goals – that I would have to race against failure never occurred to me. I'm not saying that I expected to be an 'overnight success,' I knew that the work would be long and hard, but I never thought for a moment that I wouldn't be able to take my time, go at my own speed, etc. . . . I know now that each hour is a gift – a gift that until very recently I have taken for granted and squandered recklessly – a gift that has been steadily depreciating in value because as each hour slips away it becomes increasingly unlikely that I'll be able to achieve much with what I have left – a gift I wasn't even aware I had been given, and that I frittered away because it never occurred to me that it could run out. The moment I wake up, I'm already behind. The first flush of consciousness, the first coherent rush of thought, is that I shouldn't have stayed up working so late, especially since the last couple of hours were wasted puzzling over a minor detail that I now realize, in the brutal light of day, should've been left for when I wasn't so tired, that I should've gone to sleep the moment I noticed that my thinking was becoming muddled and that I was making stupid mistakes. I should've gone to bed earlier so that when I woke up I could go back down, before I had to be at my day job, and correct that minor detail in a fraction of the time I had actually spent on it. Instead I stayed up until I was so exhausted that I couldn't even see clearly and going to sleep was more like passing out, so that when I wake up I'm already despairing over the day ahead, in particular the first eight hours I have to devote to my day job (plus two for the commute) before I can get back to the basement. I'm so overwhelmed by everything I haven't done but have promised myself *must* be done before the end of the day – although I already know that I won't even come close to getting done what I plan on doing (especially because my 'plans' are so vague and unrealistic that it's impossible to fulfill them) – that I strongly consider calling in sick and

GIVING UP

staying in bed all day. When I was younger none of my peers had accomplished much of anything, except for a few precocious ones who I wrote off as freaks of nature, outliers who weren't part of the competition. But as the years have gone by I've been watching my friends, as well as people I don't know personally but have read or heard about through mutual acquaintances, as they rack up one success after another. It's becoming difficult to categorize myself as a 'late bloomer,' since by this point most everyone I know has more or less gone through the 'blooming' phase. In fact, it's a little indecent to speak about a man my age in terms of 'blooming,' or as having bloomed. It's humiliating to think about all the stock phrases I use when I'm offering up excuses (most of the time to people who haven't asked for them) for why I haven't been able to accomplish anything yet. 'I'm a slow learner,' I say. 'Everybody develops at their own speed. I started late so I've had a lot of catching up to do. I'm not a natural like some of the other guys out there. Things don't come as easily to me as they do for some people. I just think about the work. That's all I have time for. Maybe some of the other guys are a bit cannier when it comes to that sort of thing. I'm not good at selling myself, and if you're going to make it in today's world you have to be able to sell yourself. It doesn't matter if you've come up with the best idea since sliced bread (which, in retrospect, isn't that great of an idea and likely succeeded only because somebody knew how to sell it), it doesn't matter if you're a genius, you won't have a chance in this life if you don't know how to network, bargain, convince, entice, inspire, enable, persuade, and bamboozle (like the con man). It's not enough anymore to just work hard, and I haven't figured out the other part yet. I'm not in a hurry,' I say, lying through my teeth, 'There's loads of guys like me out there who work away patiently. I'm sure it's just a matter of time.' One cliché after another. Bullshit piled on top of bullshit. The moment I utter these phrases I know that they're complete fabrications, which is not to say that they have no basis in reality – they *are* clichés after all – just that they weren't true in relation to my situation. The truth is that I haven't worked hard enough. I have been busy, but that has nothing to do with hard work. In fact, I have kept busy in order to avoid working hard. Rather than tackling problems that I've been putting off for weeks, months, years, I spend my time 'fine-tuning' parts of the work that are more or less complete and no longer require my attention, parts that have been complete for quite some time and should be left alone since my efforts to 'fine tune' usually end up undoing the work that I've already done. Even a year ago, I was much closer to completing the work than I am now. Every day that I continue to work is just one more day of ruining or undoing something that I had previously worked very hard to complete. So not only have I been wasting my time with all this busy work, but I have actually been turning back the clock, so to speak. If I could only shake off this lethargy, this apathy, this depression, and start back up with the hard work that is absolutely necessary for success, then I may still avoid the disastrous failure that looms over each passing day. But nothing seems to work. After spending the entire evening fiddling around, tinkering with a tiny detail for the thousandth time, I go to bed feeling defeated, and it's not uncommon for me to fall into total despair. As I lay there in despair over wasting yet another day – and not just wasting the day, but actually using the day to destroy what I'd already accomplished – I try to comfort myself with the thought that tomorrow will be different. Tomorrow, I vow, will mark the beginning of a renewed and revitalized effort to start back up with the serious, complicated, and exhausting work that I've basically put aside for the last year, if not longer. So the following morning, as I've already mentioned, I wake up in a panic, feeling so far behind that it's unlikely I will ever catch up. I then spend the next ten hours at my day job, and the commute to my day job, going over the resolutions from the night before and trying to decide which one I should begin with when I return to the basement. Since each resolution involves committing not just one night's worth of work, but an entire month at the very least, it's extremely important that I make the right choice. Once I decide on which resolution I'm going to start work on I will be stuck on it for at least a month and instead of the busy, mindless activity of the last year I'll be doing the hard stuff that I've been putting off in the vain hope that the work would somehow complete itself. But before I move on to the *hard* work, I say to myself as I'm heading down to the basement, I should probably start off with a few minor tasks in order to warm up, as it were, before dedicating myself to the all-consuming resolution that will monopolize my time for the foreseeable future and prevent me from working on these smaller things that require less focus, commitment, and strenuous mental effort, and that can be accomplished in a couple of hours and leave me with a sense of fulfillment, no matter how mistaken or undeserved this sensation actually is. Despite all the resolutions from the night before, I decide to start on some small, almost insignificant task. Before I can buckle down, I tell myself, I must review the work that I've accomplished thus far, so that I have a better idea of what the next step should be. I go down into the basement and start reviewing the work that I've done over the last year, and the first thought that occurs to me as I'm conducting my review is that I haven't done any work of value or substance for at least a year, maybe longer. Basically I have been wasting my time, which means I am also wasting the time of my family and friends. Whenever they have asked me about my work and have been forced to listen as I bitch and moan, complain and gripe, carrying on for hours in bitter self-pitying tones, they are having their time doubly wasted. Not only do they have to listen to the petty ramblings of a dissatisfied failure, which is a time-waster like no other, but the very basis of my complaints is completely imaginary. I talk their ears off about the insurmountable obstacles that I have to face when, in fact, no such difficulties exist because I am not really working. My friends have lost years of their lives listening to my imaginary problems with my imaginary work. But that's not even the worst part. No, the worst part, the most sad and pathetic aspect of my work in the basement, is that nobody actually cares whether I really am working or just telling people that I'm working. Aside from the annoyance, or, if they love me, the anguish, that comes with having to listen to me go on and on about some project or goal or dream that I haven't a hope in hell of realizing, and aside from the simple fact that the time spent listening to me talk about my life's work for the hundredth or even thousandth time could have been used more productively, nobody really cares what I do when I'm down in the basement, which is to say that nobody cares about the work *per se*, they care only insofar as it causes pain and distress in my life, and consequently in theirs as well. If I was already a success and had accrued some fame and accolades for accomplishments in my field, then maybe people would wonder about what I was working on. The only reason anybody cares about whether somebody is working or not is if they have already done something great and path-breaking, in which case there is good reason, or at least a reasonable possibility, to think that they may continue to do great work in the future, perhaps even greater work than what they have already accomplished. We look forward to news about their progress and wait impatiently for them to hurry up and repeat their earlier successes. And the fact that so many people care about the work this person is doing draws even more people into the anxious crowd awaiting the next installment. 'She is doing important work,' they say, and the fact that so many people are in agreement about the value of her previous work is a testament to just how important the work really is, they also say. But if we have yet to produce any work at all, whether it be important or completely insignificant, then it is quite simply impossible for anyone to give a shit one way or the other about how we spend our time, so long as it doesn't interfere with whatever they've got going on in their lives. It's not that they don't trust someone who claims to be doing great work but who hasn't produced any great work to date – it's that they *can't* trust someone who hasn't produced anything. Trust, by definition, has to be based on something (otherwise it's not trust, it's *faith*), and in the absence of any accomplished work to base it upon people can only wish you well, without being able to care what happens with the work you are allegedly slaving away on. There is no such thing as potential work, there is only accomplished work. When I've been complaining for hours about the various obstacles, both real and imaginary, that have been preventing me from completing the first phase of what I have already decided will be my life's work, and the friend or family member that has been forced to sit and listen finally interrupts me to say that they really hope that I'm able to overcome these obstacles and complete the first phase, it's entirely possible that they are telling the truth, but only in the sense that they want me to complete my work for my own sake, so I can finally stop obsessing about it and enjoy the satisfaction of accomplishing something of great and lasting importance, or for their own sake, so that they no longer have to sit through my painfully self-absorbed complaints, or, if they are a close friend, so that they don't have to watch me suffer. If I could somehow be relieved of the anguish caused by my work without having to actually complete the work itself these so-called friends of mine would be all for it. They wouldn't encourage me to keep going, to defy all the odds and everyone who had been telling me to give up. They wouldn't say, 'But you've come so far. It would be insane to stop working now after all you've done. And besides,' they wouldn't say, 'what you're doing is necessary and important.' Instead they would say, 'I don't know, maybe it's a good idea. Maybe all you need is a break, and then when you come back to it in a couple months or a year's time, you'll be refreshed and ready to work again.' Rather than spurring me on to the finish, they would wholeheartedly endorse a plan to give everything up, to simply abandon what has been the sole purpose of my life for so many years, and not because they were uncaring or cruel, but because, for them, the work did not exist in the first place. It wasn't real. When I say 'my life's work' to my friends and family, I might as well be saying 'my imaginary friend.' I might as well say, 'I spent all last night in the basement with my imaginary friend.' If they asked if they could meet my imaginary friend I would say 'not yet.' I would tell them that at that point in time it wasn't possible to see my imaginary friend. 'In fact,' I would say, 'you wouldn't even be able to see him if I showed him to you.' This is exactly what I tell people when they ask to see what I've been working on. 'You can't see it right now,' I say. 'It's too soon. It's not ready. It doesn't look like anything at this point. There's nothing to see.' The only reason anyone believes me when I tell them that I've been working on something is because there's no hard evidence against it. But it's clear that people are starting to have their doubts.

I've been talking about my work for so long, without ever giving anyone even the tiniest glimpse of what I am working on, that they're starting to question just how much work I've been doing down there in the basement. And it's a fair question, because lately, if anyone were to spy on me while I was down in the basement, they might fall under the impression that I'm not doing any work at all. For long periods at a time – not just hours, but days, and weeks, and months – I sit in the basement and do anything *but* work. Once I get home from my real job, I go down to the basement to start on my life's work, but, as I already mentioned, before I start anything new I tell myself that I need to review what I've already accomplished. Because I've been working at it for so long there are so many different aspects that I have to keep in mind at all times and the only way to do this is to review my recent work. Of course it doesn't take me very long to spot an error or a flaw, and I'm obliged to put off starting anything new until I fix it. So I work away on this until I've completely ruined everything I've already done. 'Great,' I'll say to myself. 'Just fucking great. Not only am I not getting any new work done, but I'm completely destroying everything that I've already done.' Whenever I start work, which is always very late in the day since I don't even get started until I've worked a full eight hours at my real job, I say to myself, 'Now don't go making any big decisions. In fact, don't do anything at all. Just do a quick review and pick up where you left off yesterday, then start in on the new work.' But within a few minutes I'm totally immersed, and in no time at all I become convinced that everything I've done up to that point is wrong. 'My life's work,' I say to myself, 'is a total disaster. From day one I've been heading in the wrong direction. I should start over right now. Ditch everything I've done and start fresh.' One of the big differences between me and those people you hear about who defied the odds and stuck to their guns and made their own luck is that I don't really want to succeed. If I did want to succeed, if in fact I had been telling the truth all along and had actually been devoted to success, no matter what the cost, the effect, the toll, etc., if I was really serious about my work, and not just dicking around in the basement, then wouldn't I be willing to throw it all out in order to achieve my stated goal? Of course I would. If I actually had the drive that these so-called geniuses possess, I wouldn't even hesitate. As it stands, I'm not willing to take this sort of drastic action because I don't believe that I'm capable of pulling it off. When it comes right down to it I don't have any faith in my ability to complete the project that I have devoted my life to. So instead of starting over I spend my time trying to improve upon what I've already done, which is technically impossible. The very first step I took, the very decision to start work on a project so monstrously ambitious, was the first mistake I made, and every subsequent move in that direction has been a move in the wrong direction. But now that I've gone so far in the wrong direction I have absolutely no desire to turn around and retrace my steps to where I made that first catastrophic mistake. 'It's too late,' I say to myself, 'you've gone too far. You have to see it through, even though what you're seeing through is a lifetime of mistakes.' I sit there in the basement, sunk into despair, and waste my time trying to correct a small detail, because I think that this will somehow redeem, or mask, the mountain of details that are beyond fixing, but I quickly realize that it's impossible to correct this small detail without also correcting another equally small detail. I work at correcting these minor details but I end up destroying what little value there may have been in the work I've done already, because even though these small details seem almost insignificant, and this is why they can be easily corrected (unlike the more significant, pervasive, and impossible-to-fix details), once I start making these corrections, the sheer scope of my failure is brought into sharper relief. After I have finished wasting most of my time in the basement destroying my already failed project, I force myself to stop before I've ruined everything. 'Even though what you've done so far is completely misguided and counterproductive, and the night is almost over,' I say to myself, 'it's still better than doing nothing. So just leave it alone and from now on start going in the right direction. If you start doing good work from this point on then maybe this will somehow balance out all the bad work.' I give myself a shake and check to see how much time I have left to work, and it's at this point that I realize that the night is almost over and that I have wasted it on trying to fix the unfixable, doubly wasted it in fact, because not only have I failed to improve upon my previous work, but I have actually succeeded in making it worse. And then I start panicking that there's no time left to maybe salvage something from this disaster of a workday and I decide that the best thing to do would be to take a short little break, although it's not accurate to say that *I decide to take a short break*. The truth is that even before I came down into the basement to start on my life's work I was already looking forward to the short break I would be taking once I felt as though I'd done enough to justify taking one. I am not exaggerating when I say that this break is the highlight of my day. My break is the only part of the day when I'm not completely consumed by the dread of failure. 'I deserve a break,' I think, 'even if all I've done is go over work that I should've just left alone, I've still earned this short break, and I owe it to myself to enjoy my break as much as I can before I go back and finish off the rest of the workday.' It's so important to me to use my break time as effectively as possible that often during the first shift down in the basement, while I'm doubly wasting my time ruining everything I've already accomplished, I'm also simultaneously trying to decide on what to do during my break. Most of the time I'm capable of doing both (i.e. systematically destroying my previous work and planning my break), but there are occasions when the break-planning overtakes the work-ruining so that I am completely distracted and stop working altogether in order to try to resolve what I am going to do on my break so I can go back to concentrating on destroying my past work. The reason I am so consumed by the dilemma of how to spend my break is because not only is it the only time of the day that is free of despair, but it is also the only part of the day when I allow myself to do what I really want to be doing. My whole life is one long build up to the moment when I don't have to do anything. It should almost go without saying at this point in my confession that I do not want to be working, but since I'm committed to an impossible goal and because I can't see any other way around achieving success except by ceaseless and frenzied labour, I'm left with no other choice but to spend my days doing something that I can't stand. 'I get the impression,' Mary said to me during our argument earlier today, 'that you'd be a lot happier if you weren't working down there all the time.' And when I didn't reply (because I try not to fall into these traps that she is constantly setting for me) she continued as if I hadn't heard her, or as if I might not have understood what she meant. 'It's just that it seems to make you so unhappy. The only time you seem to be relaxed and capable of enjoying yourself is when you don't have to work. I mean, do you even enjoy it?' 'Of course I do,' I said, 'why else would I be spending every waking hour working if I didn't get some sort of satisfaction out of it?' Obviously this question was meant to sound rhetorical, which is to say that it was designed to reassure Mary (and shut her up) but it was delivered without any conviction and with more than a little desperation, which is to say that it wasn't rhetorical at all. It was a straight-up question. The only answer I can think of that makes sense of why I would spend the majority of my waking hours absorbed in work that I do not enjoy, work that I may even hate, work that prevents me from achieving the everyday triumphs and goals that everyone I know who hasn't devoted themselves to some foolhardy, arrogant, ill-conceived, outdated, and impossible pursuit has been able to grasp with relative ease, because they were reasonable and attainable goals in the first place, the only reason that makes any sense is that I am working so that I can take these short breaks where I allow myself to do something that I actually enjoy doing. When I take a break from my life's work I end up doing the same sorts of things that I believe to be the pastimes of people who, since they don't live their lives devoted to an abstract and unattainable goal, live a more grounded, narrow, dim, slavish, satisfying, and rewarding day-to-day life of doing fuck all. When I was much younger and frantically trying to get my life's work under way, I didn't think that this work would involve the same variation between long periods of mundane labour punctuated by brief moments spent indulging my immediate desires and impulses that supposedly characterized the life I was trying to avoid, the unspeakably depressing fate of living for the breaks. But instead of avoiding this fate it's as though I chose the quickest route to it. Many of my friends who took the other path, the one I tried to avoid, who decided that they weren't going to waste their time chasing after a goal they could never be certain they would reach, who made a clear-eyed and deliberate decision to find a job or career that complemented their skills, talents, and character, and would allow for them to spend as much time as possible doing the things that they enjoy doing, these friends of mine, who I can hardly stand to be in the same room with, have all found that they actually enjoy the time they spend working. They have no problem going on about the pleasure they experience during their workday and confess that sometimes they don't even feel like taking a break, they just want to keep working. They're so absorbed in what they are doing that it doesn't even occur to them to take a break. Despite the fact that I've made no secret about how much trouble I have reaching the level of concentration required for the sort of demanding and complex work that I do down in the basement, and regardless of the fact that I make no effort to hide the anguished expression on my face as I'm held hostage by their enthusiasm and genuine affection for the positions that they have ended up in as a result of practical convenience, they are seemingly devoid of sympathy for my situation and go on like this for the entire dinner or cocktail or coffee or whatever the premise is that we've decided to meet under. Everything I have done, every choice I have made, has been focused on creating a life for myself that is the exact opposite of the one I am currently living. When I am out with my so-called *real* friends, the people who have, like me, devoted themselves to some open-ended, laudable, and, in most cases, artistic goal, and who, unlike me, in almost every instance have enjoyed some measure of success (although for some this is only moderate success, whereas others have achieved extremely immoderate success), we sometimes talk about the lives of our friends who *don't* live for the sake of their work but instead live for the weekend, or vacation, or their next big purchase, or simply for the health and contentment of their families – or at least this is what we imagine they live for. We talk about their lives and compare them to our own

and the tone of our conversation vacillates between conde-
scension and envy, respect and contempt, confusion and
disdain, affection and apathy. It's impossible for us to make
up our minds on what we think it means to live a life without any animating goal or *purpose*, so as soon as one of us
says, 'I wish that I could forget about my work and just kick
back and have a good time the way they do,' someone else
will say, 'But they seem really unhappy to me. They're always talking about their fucking car or their house or their
kids as if they don't know what else to say to people, which
is what happens when all you do is relax all day.' Or if someone says, 'I just can't imagine what it would be like to face
down every fucking day knowing that they're never going
to change, just one day after the other without anything to
really hold them together. You know what I mean?' then
someone will say something along the lines of, 'I know what
you mean, but I don't think it's like that for them. I think
that they like their job and they like their wife or husband
or whatever, and their kids or their pets, and they live in a
good neighbourhood and they have some close friends that
they like to hang out with and I don't think it's anymore
complicated than that. I don't think they see their life as
just one damn thing after another, to them it's just all about
being as comfortable and safe as possible and that is what
holds everything together for them.' One of us may try to
argue by saying something like, 'Yeah, but what if you're
not comfortable? Then it must feel like everything you do
is pointless?' but it's such a lame comeback that it's easy to
defend against, all you have to do is point out that 'This

isn't really any different from what we do. Some are able to pull it off, but there's loads of us out there who are miserable. For whatever reason we aren't able to succeed and it's always the same result, we end badly. And it's the same thing with them, if they can pull it off then they're happy, but if things don't go their way then they're sad and bitter and all that crap. It doesn't matter whether you devote your life to your work or just devote your life to having a good time, if things don't go your way then you're going to wish you had done things differently. The only difference between us and them is that when it works out for them they're happy, but even when it works out for us most of us are still miserable. All the joy in the world will never make us happy.' But since this particular friend of mine, the one who makes this argument, is the only one in our little group who has enjoyed the sort of success that the rest of us literally dream about, it's hard for us to listen to what he says without thinking he's being disingenuous, and that he is only making this argument because he has been so successful that he makes a big show of not valuing success at all, and attributing the good fortune of others to luck, rather than skill, in order to trivialize his own accomplishments, which of course only makes things worse. So, in an attempt to divert our attention away from the now-awkward fixation we all have on our friend's so-called success and our lack thereof, one of us will say something like, 'For me, it's not about being happy or sad or super-successful or super-depressed. You can't slice things up like that. Like, I'm a pretty miserable guy, but I can say without a doubt that I'm the happiest miserable fuck out there. Wouldn't you agree that I'm the happiest miserable guy you've ever met? You can't really say for certain that some people somehow pull it off and then live happily ever after, or that they don't pull it off so the rest of their days are a living hell. To me, what it's about is being there, you know what I mean? Like, to me, I don't care whether I pull it off or not, I just like doing it.' And it's at this point in the discussion that I'll speak up and say, 'Exactly. And that's the problem with these regular people, they are always just killing time. When they're at work they're killing time. Before they go on vacation they kill time, and even when they're on vacation they're killing time. It's like those prisoners in movies that count down the days, scratch them on the wall or X out the day on a calendar. It's like they're living their lives the way someone lives in prison. The present doesn't matter. Only what comes next matters,' I say, unsure whether I actually believe what I'm saying. Because if I stop and consider how I live my life, and think about how I spend my days, it should be immediately obvious that when I say that the problem with people is that they aren't 'living in the present,' I am actually talking about myself. I am the greatest time-killer of them all. Every waking moment of my life is murdered, by me. I strangle the life out of time. I poison it. I smother time. I beat time to a misshapen and bloody pulp. I plot against time, and then carry out my plot with ruthless cunning. In fact, whenever I am killing time I am simultaneously plotting against it. I take up a position and wait patiently for the right moment and then I make my move.

Instead of cherishing each day of my life and getting the most out of every waking moment, which is what I had intended for myself, I have systematically done away with my time. I have tried to wipe it out completely. Initially I couldn't understand why I was so compelled to kill all my time, but it suddenly came to me while I was watching a family eat dinner at one of the countless restaurants that I go to when I tell Mary that I need to go out and do something related to my life's work. If you tallied up all the hours I've spent on these so-called breaks, I'd be willing to bet that at least half have been spent at fast food restaurants – I'm not proud of this, and I don't really want to think about why I find these places so comforting, even though they are ultimately very depressing places as well. Essentially, at some point during my time-killing session in the basement, I convince myself that I might actually be able to get some work done if I went out and ate whatever I wanted. I conclude that if I indulge my perverse appetite for fast food then I'll be so satisfied that there will be nothing left to preoccupy my thoughts, since one of the reasons I find it difficult to ever get down to any serious work is because I'm always distracted by thoughts of what I would rather be doing, namely eating fast food. So it was on one of these occasions that I had just sat down to enjoy my fast food when a family took the table next to me. I could tell right away that this was going to be a noisy family, that they weren't going to just quietly go about their dinner, and I was annoyed that they'd chosen the table next to me when there were plenty of empty ones on the other side of the restaurant. It was obvious that their kids had been poorly brought up. I could see it in their frantic, unblinking faces. And it was just as obvious that the parents had relinquished all but the most basic responsibility and affection for these little kids, and that short of causing physical damage to the tables and/or chairs or injuring one of the patrons in the restaurant, they weren't going to try to control them. As the family sat down at the table next to me the boys were already in tears. From what I could make out they were upset because they didn't want to eat the dinner that their parents had purchased for them. It seemed that despite the parents' unquestionable lack of interest in their children's well-being, they hadn't succumbed to absolute depravity, because even though those almost feral young boys insisted that they didn't want burgers for dinner and wanted ice cream instead, their parents refused to oblige them. And when they went from crying to the first stages of throwing a tantrum, their mom said that if they didn't stop acting like a bunch of babies and eat their goddamn food that there wouldn't be any ice cream for dessert. Without a word of protest, the boys started to eat their food, but they did it quickly and joylessly. I sat there with my own food growing colder on the tray as I watched these two kids joylessly consume food that I considered to be delicious, even if it was in many ways revolting, just so they could get to the food that they really wanted to be eating, which didn't appeal to me at all. (I don't have much of a sweet tooth.) The reason that I went to that particular fast food restaurant was because I liked to eat the burgers they served. You could say that my goal for my break was to eat burgers at that restaurant. The boys wanted ice cream, not burgers. Ice cream was their goal. So when they were forced to eat burgers in order to get ice cream they bolted the burgers into their mouths and chewed and swallowed, more or less racing through their meal, killing it basically. It occurred to me that this is how I approached my life's work in the basement. I was just like those greedy boys in the restaurant – instead of savouring the time I spent in the basement I approached each night of work with the same resentment as they did when they choked down their burgers. My goal was to finish my life's work, not to spend my life working on my life's work. In fact, I saw the time I had to spend in the basement as an obstacle to successfully completing my life's work, which, of course, doesn't make any sense at all. Every time I make the trip down into the basement, I always try to think of an alternative that might save me from having to work, something that is equally integral to my goal, but that will keep me upstairs for the night. I was thrilled whenever some bureaucratic task came along – whether it was filling out a form or placing a phone call – and I treated these bureaucratic chores as though they were as important as the work I was doing in the basement, while I treated the basement work as if it were an annoying and time-wasting bureaucratic task. The amount of care and effort that I put into filling out a more or less insignificant form, or the level of thought and consideration that would go into even the most prosaic phone call, was much much greater than what I was willing to commit when it came to the basement

GIVING UP

work. And this is for me perhaps the most shameful of the many shameful secrets I keep from Mary. She repeatedly insists that she doesn't mind how much time I spend down in the basement working away on something that simply doesn't exist for her. She insists that it makes no difference to her whether I succeed or fail, and if it weren't for the fact that she was finding it increasingly difficult to be the primary breadwinner and housekeeper in our apartment (my real job didn't pay well) while I wasted my time doing something that – from her perspective – I didn't even appear to enjoy, then she would have *no problem* with whatever I wanted to do with my *free time*. 'What I want to know,' she often says, as a preamble to a question that to me is entirely irrelevant, 'is whether you even like doing what you're doing?' And even though I think that whether I enjoy the basement work is beside the point, I can't help but feel ashamed when I tell her that I do enjoy my life's work, because the truth is that I don't, which is why I look forward to taking a break, because not only do I finally allow myself something that I really want, but I also allow myself to stop doing something that I really don't want to be doing. Tonight, when it was finally time for me to take my break, I found myself paralyzed with indecision. Once my break was over I was going to have to return to the basement and resume my work, and since I had vowed to myself that I wouldn't waste any more time reviewing/ruining the work that I had already accomplished and would start in on new work, I was particularly anxious that I would spend my break doing something especially enjoyable and satisfying.

But the pressure to choose an activity that could meet these requirements made it impossible to decide on anything at all. Mary and I still hadn't made up over our fight after she got home from work, so when I came up from the basement and saw the glow from the computer, I walked past without saying anything to her, and since she didn't say anything to me I left without telling her where I was going, and I found myself wandering the streets in a state of aimless despair. 'Not only am I wasting my time trying to achieve something that is simply not within me to achieve,' I said to myself, 'but I even waste the time I set aside without any other goal than to enjoy myself.' I live in what can only be described as a *lively neighbourhood*, and even though it wasn't very late and the weather was mild – the ideal weather for an evening stroll – the streets surrounding my home were surprisingly deserted. Even though literally thousands of people live in my neighbourhood, not one of them was out for a stroll, or an errand, or even just to stand on their front step or patio or balcony and stare at the clear night sky and enjoy what I considered to be unseasonably warm weather. I felt as though the neighbourhood had evacuated and that I was the only person left because I'd been too busy at my life's work to notice this mass flight. This may be why, when I saw a man standing on the corner just ahead of me, I didn't turn around or cross the street to avoid him, which is what I normally would have done. Instead, when he turned to see me coming and raised a hand in greeting, I raised my hand in response and headed directly for him. Under any other circumstances, I would've been overcome with dread at the prospect of encountering a stranger, not out of fear for my safety but because, in my experience, the only reason a stranger ever wants to introduce himself is because they want something from you, and since I had no desire to give away what little time and money I had, I shouldn't even have acknowledged him. It was a waste of time for the both of us. Our encounter would surely end in disappointment, but I was in a desperate state, and at the sight of this guy on the corner I decided to ignore all my prejudices against strangers and to go see what he wanted. I was immediately impressed by his good looks. It's altogether rare that a stranger who approaches someone on the street is anything other than decidedly unattractive, at the very least, and usually kind of scary. I'll admit that the stranger's good looks temporarily confused me. Even as he was calling out to me in a hoarse and strained voice and coming towards me at a near sprint, obviously worried that I might drop eye contact and revert to the blank pedestrian stare, I was too absorbed in scrutinizing his remarkable features to notice just how fucked up this guy actually was, but by the time we were facing each other and he asked me if I could do him a *really big favour* I'd become aware of how his handsome features had clearly been ruined by what I assumed was a pretty serious drinking problem, and when I looked closer into the glacial tint of his eyes it occurred to me that there may be other factors involved in the decline of his good looks aside from alcohol. *There was no doubt in my mind that I was being approached by someone who was after my money.* Since he came to me, instead of waiting for me to pass by, I knew that he wasn't going to come right out and ask for it. He was going to try to tell me a story that would pin me down and make it difficult for me to interrupt him to say that I didn't have any money, because then he'd get all offended and claim that I didn't let him finish, and that if I had, I would've known that he was, in fact, not asking me for money. In fact, the opposite was true, he was offering to give *me* money. The peremptory way he had raised his hand, the panic in his eyes, the desperate tone of his voice, the ruin of what must've been, only a little while ago, fine, youthful features, everything about his approach that betrayed just how shifty and potentially dangerous this stranger was, all of this was immediately clear to me as I stood listening to him relate the elaborate story that he'd come up with in order to con me out of my money. 'I have this money order,' he said, and flashed a form in my face as if he wanted me to examine it so I could see for myself that he wasn't lying. But when I leaned in for a closer look at what did in fact appear to be a standard triplicate money order form (not that I'd ever seen a money order form before he showed me his, but it seemed likely that what he had was the real thing), he quickly stuffed it in his pocket and continued with his story as if the authenticity of the money order form had been definitively established. 'My car is in the fucking impound lot,' he smiled here, the way a prisoner might smile at his new cellmate, the sort of smile that implies a shared fate. 'Can you believe it? I'm parked at my girlfriend's,' he gestured vaguely up the street, 'and thought that at worst they might give me a ticket, not tow the fucking thing.' I was nodding along impatiently to what he was saying. I'd finally decided that at the first chance to interrupt I was going to tell him that I had somewhere I needed to be, that I was late, and that even if I wanted to help him out, it wasn't going to happen. But it was at the mention of his girlfriend that I felt the first surge of the anxiety that would bother me for the remainder of our encounter. I knew that everything he was saying was a lie, but until he mentioned his girlfriend I was happy to stand there and let him lie to me. It didn't matter to me whether the story he was telling was true or false because at that particular moment I just wanted to listen to someone else tell me a story, as long as it was plausible, which is to say that I didn't believe what he was saying, but it was still important that what he was saying was believable. But at that point, while I was standing there listening to him feed me a line of complete bullshit, even after I had just resolved on breaking off the encounter, I changed my mind and gave up on the idea of interrupting him, of bringing his preposterous story to an abrupt end and going on down the street to some all-night café or diner where I could take my break in peace, and then head back to the basement to continue my life's work. One moment I was disinterestedly listening to what he was saying but mostly thinking about how I could get away from this guy, and the next I was actually listening to what he was telling me. Even though I knew his story was bullshit, I started to listen as if it were real. I could see his car in the lot, I could see his girlfriend back at her apartment, asleep in a single bed. I know this doesn't make any sense, that it shouldn't be possible to know that something isn't true while simultaneously believing that it is, but I don't know how else to explain what I was feeling as I stood there listening to the stranger. 'And me, being the genius that I am, left my bag in my car that had my laptop and wallet, basically my entire fucking life. I know,' he said, while staring directly into my eyes as if he was trying to see what sort of effect his story was having, whether I was *buying it*, 'I'm a fucking idiot, right? It gets worse. I don't live here, you see? I just came down to see my girlfriend. I work for a mining company up north. You know St. James Bay? No? Well it's like five hours north. I live in a camp. Stuck up there with a bunch of guys just like me. So any chance I get I'm down here with my girlfriend. You know what I'm saying? Beats getting drunk and listening to a bunch of guys jerk off in your tent, if you catch my drift.' I nodded to show that I understood what he meant. There was something about this part of his story that had the flavour of truth to it or the ring of truth – *the aura* – as though what he was saying was based on experience, but it was only partial, a feeling or an impression, as if something about the original experience had been altered or excised. Maybe what he was telling me would have been more convincing if it hadn't seemed so important to him that I sign off on this aspect of his story, but even though I was no longer looking for an opportunity to cut him off and extricate myself from this situation, I was impatient for him to wrap things up and get to the point in his story where he asked me for money. 'So I had a day off, literally twenty-four hours, and I burned down here to get a little action so that I don't lose my fucking mind. What happens? My fucking car gets towed,' he was getting worked up, as if, like me, he actually believed what he was saying, even though he knew better than I did that everything he'd been telling me was a lie. 'And if I'm not back at camp in ten hours I'm going to lose my job.' He paused. This was the crucial point in his story where he would have to make the transition from explaining his predicament to explaining what I could do to help. He knew that if I didn't believe the first part of the story that there was no way I was going to hear him out during the next part, especially since he was going to be asking me for something I would likely be very reluctant to give away. This was why he'd gone through the trouble of creating a bunch of entirely probable details – the mining camp in St. James Bay, the towed car with his wallet and laptop locked inside, the long lonely drive (five hours each way) in order to get his rocks off with his girlfriend, the tent full of drunk, masturbating men – that were largely extraneous to the main plot, which was that he was stuck here without any means of getting back to his job. He could've said to me, 'I'm not from here and I need money to get back to where I'm from.' But he knew that if he approached me like that then I wouldn't even have bothered to come up with an excuse for why I couldn't help him out, that I would've simply ignored him and kept walking. The only way I was going to stand there and listen to him was if he made up a bunch of elaborate lies. If I tell you that I own a dog then the only reason you have to believe me is that it would be pointless to lie about something like that. You don't believe in the dog. You believe in me. But if I tell you that I own a small Irish Setter, that it's more my wife's dog than mine, but that I still like to take him for walks, that he can't wag his tail because after only having him for a year he got out one day and ran into the road that runs past our front yard where he got hit by some maniac who didn't even bother to stop, but luckily all that happened was that he lost the ability to wag his tail, if I told you that he didn't actually look like an Irish Setter, that he was smaller than most dogs of that breed and his hair shorter and not very red, but that we got him from a breeder just out of town and he was definitely purebred, if I loaded on all this detail, even if none of it was true (in particular, the very claim that I owned a dog of any kind) you would find it hard not to believe me, and not just because I hadn't given you a reason to doubt what I was saying – why would I lie about having a dog? – but also because by inventing these circumstantial details I made the dog real for you. Even if, after telling you I owned a dog, and relating all these imaginary details about my imaginary dog, I confessed that I actually didn't own a dog, you would have a hard time believing that my dog didn't exist. You would know that this Irish Setter was a complete fabrication, because I told you that it was, but once I'd planted the image of a brown, squat, short-haired gun-dog with a paralyzed tail, it would be almost impossible to erase. This is what the stranger (who had in fact introduced himself by name, though this was before I'd been listening to him) was trying to do by burying me in all this detail when he could've just hit me up for cash. 'By the time I finish telling my story,' he must've thought, 'there's no way he'll be able to turn me down.' But even after relating this elaborate lie he was still worried that I wouldn't believe him, which, of course, most people wouldn't have. If it was anybody else, they would've caught on at his very first lie ('I have this money order') and everything he said afterwards, all his carefully chosen embellishments, would have struck them as completely ridiculous. But when he first approached me, brandishing the money order and piling on some elaborate bullshit about his car being impounded, I was still distracted by thoughts of how to spend my break, what I should do to make the most of my trips away from the work that was going so poorly, and my life upstairs, which wasn't going all that well either. Then, gradually, I started to pay attention, and then all at once I found myself listening to what he was saying and believing what he was saying, as if what he'd been saying was actually true, which, of course, I knew wasn't. If I was just standing there listening to him because I was desperate for a distraction, something to keep me away from the basement, or because I was too much of a coward to interrupt him and tell him to fuck off, or because I was so absorbed in my own thoughts about how I was wasting my time in the basement and destroying what little I'd managed to accomplish, or if I was actually taken in by his bullshit story of having his car towed, then there would be nothing more remarkable about what happened to me than any of the other poor fools out there who are cheated out of their hard-earned money, either because they're not paying attention, they lack the nerve, or they're simply not all that sharp. What's strange about my case is that I knew that the stranger was full of shit, but I believed he was telling the truth – I knew that he was trying to cheat me out of my money, I knew that all I had to do was walk away, but I also knew that I wasn't going to. It's like in *Don Quixote*. At the beginning of the book Alonso Quixano suffers an attack of madness and decides to dress as a knight errant and go around the Andalusian countryside having the sort of adventures that he'd been reading about all his life in the romances he was more or less addicted to. Because Alonso lives in the real world, and not the world of literary courtly romance, his experiment is a disaster, and at numerous points throughout the story it seems likely that Alonso is going to lose his life on account of the savage beatings he suffers at the hands of people he mistakes for characters in the demented courtly romance playing out in his mind. But no matter how savage these beatings are, he holds on to his illusions. Even when his companion, Sancho Panza, who suffers from something much more banal (i.e. credulousness) but that certainly afflicts more people than madness, repeatedly attempts to disabuse Alonso of some of his more dangerous delusions – the chief one being that Alonso, who is described at the beginning of the book as bordering on fifty, in a time when living past sixty was a sort of minor miracle, is not in any shape to be riding around and challenging barbers, shepherds, biscainers (?), and in one famous instance, a windmill, to duel to the death – Alonso (as Don Quixote) comes up with some explanation that allows him to persist in his insane adventure as knight errant while conceding to Sancho's reasoning. In fact, at the end of the novel, Alonso is lying on his deathbed and all at once his madness clears – 'my judgment is now undisturbed, and free from those dark clouds of ignorance with which my eager and continual reading of those detestable books of chivalry had obscured it' – and at the hour of his death he repents for the whole knight errant thing ('I must confess I have been a madman.'). He gathers all his friends in the hope of redeeming himself ('not to leave the imputation of madness on my memory') but they justifiably suspect that 'some new frenzy had possessed him.' And, in their defense, after a thousand pages of Alonso as Don Quixote, it's easy to understand why everyone, especially Sancho Panza, is a bit disappointed by Alonso as Alonso. But this isn't why the end of the book is so disturbing. What I couldn't get over was that Alonso could remember everything he did as Don Quixote, whereas I would've expected that when a character literally loses his mind, and that mind is replaced with a new mind (the mad mind), then if he ever managed to recover his old mind again (his *real* mind) it seems to make sense that he would have to give up the mad mind and all the memory that went with it, so that all that would remain of that period of madness would be a shadow that covered everything in darkness ('those dark clouds of ignorance'). But Alonso remembers everything he did as Don Quixote, in fact, he even makes good on promises he had made to Sancho Panza, even though it would've been understandable if, since he was no longer crazy, those commitments were considered null and void, though it would've been a bit cheap of him. It seemed to me that at the end Alonso was of two minds, the sane and the mad, and that even as he looked back over his adventures as the mad Don Quixote, from the now sane perspective of Alonso, he hadn't lost the illusions of his former self, so that when it came time for his confession he repented of his madness and folly, rejecting the stories and books that corrupted his mind, yet did not go so far as to renounce his past – 'I was Don Quixote de la Mancha,' he says, 'I am now, as I have said, the good Alonso Quixano.' I had always assumed that it was impossible to be of two minds, that once you went crazy it was no longer possible to keep one foot in the door that opened onto reality, and that what people meant when they used this clumsy expression was that within the one and only mind in their possession a distance had opened up between two points and they didn't have the will, or the strength, or the courage of their convictions to make a move in either direction. When Alonso says, 'I am no longer Don Quixote de la Mancha,' to me it was as if he was saying that he had *never been Don Quixote*, that throughout the entire novel I had been reading about a gentleman who was only pretending to be mad, when he had been sober-minded the entire time (even though pretending to be insane is its own form of madness). In one interpretation we have a gentleman who reads so many books that he is *driven mad*, and in another interpretation we have a gentleman who reads so many books that he *decides* to go mad. But Alonso's deathbed confession introduces the possibility of a third interpretation, where someone reads so many books that his mind splits in two, and that even when he was completely mad the *real* mind was also always present, and once his *real* mind returns to the forefront, the madness recedes, but never goes away. 'This is why,' I thought, 'even when Alonso is engaging in one of Don Quixote's mad adventures he does it in a very deliberate and *self-conscious* way, as if he was a sane person imitating a crazy person.' And I found this much more disturbing than the possibility of losing one's mind, because it suggested that it was possible for someone to be crazy and sane at the exact same time. 'This is what I'm doing right now,' I thought, 'while I stand here listening to this con man try to cheat me out of my money.' At the same time that I knew this guy was a complete fake, and not even a good fake, because within seconds of our encounter I could tell that he was lying – the moment he said, 'I have this money order,' I knew for a fact that what he held in his hand was a fake money order – I also believed (or, to be precise, another 'I' believed, different from the 'I' that didn't) that he was telling me the truth. Either way, whether he was lying or telling the truth, I could interrupt him at any point and tell him that I couldn't help him out. Even though I had been hearing him out, there was nothing preventing me from bringing this encounter to a premature end. Just like when I was working in the basement, there was nothing keeping me there except for my will, or lack thereof, to remain. The stranger hadn't grabbed onto me, or backed me up against a wall, and, while it was late and the streets were deserted, he hadn't done anything to indicate that the encounter might turn violent. He hadn't even said that I 'had to help him,' that he had 'no one else to turn to,' that I was his 'last hope' and that if I didn't help him out he didn't know 'what he would do.' He may have seemed desperate, but so far his desperation had only manifested itself as a willingness to lie and cheat people out of their hard-earned money. There was no indication that he was desperate enough to try to rob me, by attacking me or threatening to attack me. It seemed to me that if I did decide to interrupt him and say that I was sorry, that I wished I was able to help him, but that I was only out for a stroll and that I had to hurry back home, he wouldn't even make a fuss. 'I bet that if I just cut him off right now he'll let me leave without putting up much of a fight,' I thought. 'He's probably embarrassed by his transparently amateur attempt at a con and once I indicate that I know what he's up to he'll be in as much of a hurry to get away from me as I am to get away from him.' Since I was embarrassed by his attempt to cheat me out of my money I assumed that he would be at least equally, although likely more so, as embarrassed as I was. 'This must be what it's like for my friends and family,' I thought. 'They must get embarrassed when they have to listen to me go on about my life's work. They know that I'm lying when I tell them that I think I'll finish the project that I'm currently working on in another year or so. It's painfully obvious to my wife that I am conning her, putting one over on her, so to speak, when, after a doubly wasteful and destructive day down in the basement, I tell her that I got a lot of work done. It's embarrassing to listen to someone lie to you once it's been established that you know they are lying and they know that you know they are lying,' I thought. 'They're embarrassed because you are obliging them to pretend (to play make-believe) that something is real that they know for a fact to be fake, which, to some degree, makes them complicit in the deception. They're embarrassed because, like you, they don't want to face the reality of the situation, and prefer to hang on to the illusion, even though they are perfectly aware that it is just that, an illusion,' I thought. 'But maybe this means that on some level they believe the illusion is real, and they're embarrassed for hanging on to this paradox. They're embarrassed because I'm obliging them to have faith in something (i.e. my life's work) that they know I don't even have faith in.' And so my embarrassment increased once the stranger began to make the transition from the set-up of his elaborate but amateurish story about having his car towed, to his pitch (i.e. how I could help him out). 'So here I am, locked out of my girlfriend's apartment. I have no idea how to get ahold of her. She's at work at some bar I don't even know the name of and I don't even know which building she's in. So I called one of my buddies at the camp and he sent me this money order, but since I don't have any ID they won't let me cash it. I asked them,' he said, 'why the fuck do I need a money order, right? Like obviously if I had my wallet and ID and shit then I wouldn't need my buddy to wire me cash, would I?' He was staring at me now, wildly, no doubt channelling a recent customer service altercation to make his performance believable, getting angry as he reflected on this unrelated outrage and raising his voice so that I nodded along in agreement in order to quiet him down. 'For sure,' I said. 'That's ridiculous.' And although I was placating him by commiserating over the alleged policies of the alleged FedEx outlet, I was also trying to hurry things along and get to the point, so when I said 'That's ridiculous,' I was also implicitly saying, 'I get it. The modern world is a cold, impersonal, irrational nightmare populated by uncaring people. I see that you are in a precarious situation and the only person who can help you from losing your job is me. So just make your request and I will decide whether I want to help you or not, but please don't keep telling me every detail of your predicament or I'm going to lose my patience and leave.' Unfortunately I must've done a bad job of communicating this subtext because from what I could tell, instead of interpreting my remark – 'That's ridiculous' – as a sign to wrap up his preamble and move on to the con, he clearly took my remark as encouragement to relate even more inconsequential details about the imaginary FedEx outlet. He chose to interpret my remark as an expression of solidarity, like I was saying, 'Go ahead. You've found a kindred spirit and sympathetic ear. I too am the victim of bureaucratic incompetence and the crass indifference of the general public. If you were looking for someone who could share in your anguish over the daily insults of living in this ass-backwards shambles that passes for civilization then look no further. I'm your man.' So he told me that the woman who was serving him was 'Paki, or something like that,' and that he could hardly understand what she'd been saying to him 'in the first place' and that when he'd asked to speak with the manager she revealed that she was, in fact, the manager. 'Can you fucking believe that?' he asked. 'I'm not being racist, but how does somebody who can hardly speak the language get to be the manager at a place where their job is to talk to customers all day?' I nodded even though I was offended by what he was saying, not because I was uncomfortable with racism (which, truth be told, I wasn't, and the only time I was sensitive about that sort of thing was when I was in the presence of a visible, or invisible, minority – something that, consequently probably makes me more than a little bit of a racist) but because it seemed presumptuous of him to assume that I wouldn't be offended by what he was saying (a lot of people would have been). 'What makes him so sure that he can open up to me like this,' I thought, 'and say something that would be considered racist in most circles?' So I finally interrupted him and brought his elaborate preamble to a close, 'They wouldn't give you the money?' 'Not a chance,' he said. 'You should've seen me. Let's just say that after what I said to her I don't think it'd be a good idea for me to go back there.' Even though he had developed this story in the greatest detail and I was now fully apprised of every aspect of his 'situation,' I could tell that he was still reluctant to make his request, as if he wasn't interested in conning me out of my money anymore. He was absorbed in the storytelling process and I got the impression that as he was telling his story he'd become increasingly determined that I actually believe what he was telling me, regardless of whether it was true or not, and that it wasn't even necessary for me to give him any money so long as I kept listening. But this probably wasn't the case. I was likely projecting my insecurities onto him. Whatever anxiety he was exhibiting had nothing to do with whether I believed in him. It was because now there was nothing left to do but pull off his con. Now he was only seconds away from finding out whether his bullshit story had been a success or a failure, whether he had reached his goal (i.e. somebody gullible enough to be cheated out of their money) or whether I was going to turn him down, leaving him right where he began, having accomplished nothing. 'But what really pissed me off,' he finally explained, 'is that if I had my wallet I wouldn't even need any ID because then I'd have my ATM card.' I asked him why he didn't get a temporary replacement card and he paused for a second as he was either remembering the reason, or trying to invent one. 'Cause you need ID for that,' he assured me, obviously pleased with himself for coming up with something in time. 'These things,' he said, brandishing the money order, 'are like cheques. It's true,' he said in earnest, even though I hadn't done anything to indicate that I doubted what he was saying, 'they work the same way a cheque does. You can deposit them at a bank machine the same way you do a regular cheque,' he said, again with the wild stare, daring me to contradict him, but I wasn't paying attention because now that I knew the nature of his request (i.e. that he wasn't going to ask for whatever money I had on my person but instead he was planning on getting me to withdraw money from my bank account) I was able to start working on an airtight excuse that would let me refuse him without indicating that I thought that what he had told me was complete bullshit. He could sense that he was losing me so he hurried through the rest. 'It's made out to me so I sign the back and you sign here,' he pointed to the form but he was still holding it out of reach and I couldn't make out what he was pointing at, 'then you cash it like an EI cheque. It's five hundred so I sign it over to you then you take out four hundred and keep a hundred for yourself.' By the time he got to the last sentence he was speaking so quickly I almost didn't understand what he'd said, and it took me a moment to realize that he had finally made his proposal. It was so tossed off, as if it wasn't really significant to the rest of the story, certainly not as significant as the fact that the manager of the FedEx outlet was Pakistani or Indian (or neither, perhaps). Obviously he didn't expect me to believe anything he'd just said and even if I did, what were the odds that I would be willing to go to a bank machine and withdraw four hundred dollars and hand it over to him? By the time he finally made his request he seemed to have more or less given up and he had a look of bitter sadness, but also relief, the look people get when something they've been dreaming of ends in disappointment, and even though they never really thought it would happen they're surprised by how crushed they are when it doesn't, but relieved that they no longer have to hope for it. Why wouldn't he just hit me up for a smaller sum, which I might actually be willing to give to him, instead of going for so much, essentially guaranteeing that I would refuse, say 'no way in hell,' tell him to go fuck himself, or something along those lines? It didn't make any sense. It was a completely ridiculous expectation on his part that he'd be able to con a stranger out of four hundred dollars with his albeit credible story of having his car towed (which happened all the time in this city, although since it was so common an occurrence there was something clichéd, and therefore, incredible, about his story). 'Wouldn't it make more sense,' I thought, 'to hit people up for twenty or thirty bucks so that, whether they believed his bullshit story about getting his car impounded, they may just fork over the cash in order to shut him up and get him to leave them alone, and if he put in a good eight-hour day and covered enough ground it's more than possible that he'd eventually cheat and con enough strangers that he'd end up with four hundred, instead of going around and, once he finally built up the nerve to make what was obviously a desperate and foolish proposal, pouring out his long drawn-out story only to be told there *was nothing they could do for him*. 'What he's trying to do,' I thought, 'is completely unrealistic.' It struck me as so unrealistic that I started to consider the possibility that he was telling the truth. I've already remarked that he was good looking, and on top of that he was well dressed, not that he was 'dressed up,' just that the clothes he had on were of good quality, clean, and in decent condition. He spoke well, with a slight accent, and his voice was strong and distinctive, as if he would've been comfortable on stage or behind a microphone. If it weren't for the fact that he was hitting me up for four hundred bucks then he would've been the sort of person that I often find myself admiring when I pass them on the sidewalk, or stand next to them in an elevator, or sit next to them in a movie theatre – tall, ruggedly handsome, and (I've always assumed) successful in both the professional and private realms. But here was one of these sorts, one of these people that I would've normally envied, looking wild in the eye, talking excitedly, and basically coming off as a total junkie. In fact, when I looked at the situation from this perspective, it became increasingly plausible that this guy was for real. Otherwise he would've tried a less ambitious course of action. If he was the sort of person who goes through life as the object of envy for people like me then it's not so unlikely that he would approach a stranger and expect them to be willing to fork over four hundred bucks, because it might not occur to him that anyone would ever suspect that he was something other than what he appeared to be. All at once I changed my mind. I was being paranoid instead of seeing what would've been obvious to most everyone else, that this stranger was telling me the truth. I only saw my own cynical and paranoid image of the stranger, one that was wholly incommensurate with who he actually was. Why else would he be willing to ask for four hundred dollars if he hadn't been telling the truth? And he wasn't even asking for four hundred dollars. He was actually proposing that I cash his five hundred dollar money order and keep one hundred for myself. He wasn't trying to cheat me out of four hundred dollars at all, in fact, this ruggedly handsome man was willing to give me one hundred dollars for the trouble of cashing a money order that he, due to a confluence of circumstances that he couldn't have foreseen, was unable to cash. Miners can make a lot of money, and it wasn't so far-fetched that he would throw a hundred my way to do something that was only a minor inconvenience for me, whereas for him it was a big deal. 'Can I see the money order?' I said. He looked at the form in his hand and then he looked at me. He seemed worried, although I wasn't sure if this was because the money order was bogus and by handing it over he was going to lose his opportunity to screw me out of four hundred dollars, or if, since the money order was legit, he was actually worried that *I* couldn't be trusted, that *I* was not what I seemed to be, and that if he handed over the money order I might try to take off with it and keep the full five hundred bucks for myself. He stood alongside me and held the money order in front of us so that I could inspect it up close, and even take hold of the opposite corner, while he could be sure that at any second he could snatch it from my view. 'See,' he said, 'it's pretty standard.' I, as I've already mentioned, had never seen a money order form before. They might as well have been from the same era as telegrams or trunk calls (whatever the hell they were), which is to say I considered them to be antiquated, obsolete, and so I certainly wasn't in a position to judge whether the form he held out in front of me was standard or not. 'That's my friend,' he said, and pointed to a line near the top of the form where in faint blue ink someone had written the name 'Gary Trites.' If he was trying to con me out of four hundred dollars then he was taking a big risk by letting me inspect the money order form.

For all he knew, I might be the sort of person that regularly deals with money orders, and so knows what a legitimate form would look like. 'There's no way he'd try to pass a bogus form off on someone like me,' I thought, and when I thought 'someone like me' what I meant was a relatively well-dressed, normal-looking, intelligent-seeming man – my intelligence, I believed, would have been evident to the stranger within seconds of our encounter – but I might as well have thought 'someone like him,' since I considered him to be well-dressed, good-looking, and obviously intelligent (or intelligent-seeming, at least) even though the desperate and wild eyes that were fixed on me throughout his whole story made me think of the senile patients at a nursing home. He had a nice voice and spoke clearly in full sentences and without the usual pauses, repetitions, and abrupt transitions and loopy syntax that characterize what passes for speech these days. He didn't saturate his story with obscenities or any of the other commonplace verbal tics. And if it weren't for his crazed and hollow stare I wouldn't have doubted that I was speaking with someone in possession of a keen intellect. But the way that he was looking at me as he kept pointing at the name on the form and repeating the blank assertion 'That's my friend', suggested that he wasn't 'all there', or that he was a bit 'off.' 'Either way,' I thought, 'he'd have to be pretty stupid to think that someone like me wouldn't be able to tell the difference between a phony money order and a real one. Why would he risk showing me the money order unless it was the real thing?' I scanned the rest of the form and even though I had never seen one before I decided right away that it was legit. The FedEx logo was featured on the top left and the rest was divided into the boxed grid you would expect from the sort of form designed to record and transfer a sum of money. In addition to this, the form was a colour-coded sequence of three sheets with two carbon inserts, and it seemed altogether unlikely that this guy would have been able to forge this style of document, since the materials aren't available to general consumers and would've had to have been ordered from some sort of specialized merchant who dealt in carbon triplicate forms and that sort of thing. I focussed on the text and was immediately struck by the words 'Money Order' on the top of the form. I was so intent on determining the authenticity of the form that it didn't occur to me that he could have stolen it, or that they might be freely available to anyone coming in off the street. 'See,' he said, following my gaze and indicating a line just below the title where $500 had been scrawled in pale blue ink. 'It's like a cheque.' Now that I was convinced that it was legitimate, I began to pay closer attention to what was written in the little boxes, but aside from 'Gary Trites' and '$500' the form was blank except for another name – 'Luke MacDonald' – and an illegible signature at the bottom. 'Is that you?' I asked, pointing at the signature. 'Yeah,' he said, pulling the form away and putting out his hand for me to shake it. 'Sorry, didn't I give you my name?' It's Luke.' I shook his hand as impersonally as I could manage. 'Okay, Luke,' I said, 'let's go cash this money order.' This had the effect of taking him completely by surprise, so much that before I'd finished saying 'let's go cash this money order,' he'd already started to respond defensively, as if to a question or an accusation. It was clear that he hadn't been listening to what I was saying, only that I was saying something, and he assumed (reasonably enough) that I was going to say something about how the form was blank except for his friend's name, the sum, his name, and his signature. Shouldn't there be something else? More information? At some point he registered what I'd said but it was as though he kept going because he was so shocked by my abrupt acceptance. It took a moment, but when he finally did stop talking he stood in front of me and stared. He'd been prepared for failure. The moment he approached me he probably said to himself, 'There's no way this guy is going to listen to me, and even if I do manage to get him to stop and hear me out, there's no way he's going to believe a word I say.' The reason he seemed so desperate was because he knew how ridiculous it was to expect someone to hear him out, believe his story, and then go through the trouble of depositing the money order in their account so they could withdraw four hundred and hand it over. This was why he'd been willing to approach a complete stranger and humiliate himself with an outrageous request. 'I've got nothing to lose,' he probably thought. It's not that he didn't hope to succeed, he wouldn't have bothered approaching me in the first place if that was the case, it was just that he never suspected it would really happen. To put it in more simple terms, he knew he wasn't going to succeed, but he wasn't going to stop approaching strangers until he did. So he couldn't believe his luck (and that's what it was, luck) when the impossible finally happened and I agreed to cash the money order at the bank machine a couple blocks away. After standing there silently and staring at me in utter disbelief he appeared to accept the fact that I had agreed to help him out and suddenly hurried to thank me, piling on the gratitude, going on about how he 'could tell right away that I was a good guy' and that I was basically saving his life. He'd started walking in the direction of the bank machine and while he kept heaping on the compliments he suddenly became impatient. While he'd been telling me his story he stared at me the entire time, but now he was looking all around him as if he was expecting someone to show up right at that moment, someone that he'd forgotten about and only just remembered. I had expected him to be grateful, but his non-stop praise was so over the top (at one point he compared me to Jesus) and he was so overwhelmed and pathetic, that it struck me as suspicious. In fact, what bothered me about the way he was carrying on was that he was behaving as though I had agreed to *give* him four hundred dollars, instead of agreeing to cash his money order and take one hundred dollars of his money for my trouble. It was like he'd forgotten everything he'd just told me about the money order (if only for a second), like once I said 'let's go cash this money order' he'd been so surprised, so completely caught off guard, that he forgot to remember that I was doing him a small favour, one that I was supposedly going to profit from, and that it was really just a minor inconvenience (if, that is, his story had been true, which, of

GIVING UP

course, it wasn't) and so he felt the same gratitude that anyone would feel if, out of desperation, they were obliged to ask a complete stranger for four hundred dollars and on account of some fucked-up luck the stranger said 'Sure! I'll give you four hundred dollars.' He sensed that something was off. He didn't believe me, but since I didn't refuse him outright he couldn't plead his case any further, so he tried to steer the conversation towards innocuous bullshit about where I was from, since he assumed (correctly) that I wasn't from around here. I answered his questions as if I was taking an exam, which is to say that I answered immediately, without thinking about what I was saying, because all I was thinking about was how I was going to get away from this guy. 'I'm not going to go through with this,' I thought, 'Even though I said I would there is no way that I'm going to hand over four hundred bucks to this guy. There's still time for me to do something before we get to the bank machine. I can think of some excuse to get me out of this mess.' So even as I was telling this stranger about my childhood I was frantically searching for a reason for why I wouldn't be able to give him four hundred dollars without, at the same time, revealing that the reason I couldn't deposit the money order was because I didn't believe a word of what he'd said. 'Because that's what you're doing,' I said to myself, 'you are giving this guy four hundred dollars out of your own pocket, and making a fraudulent deposit, which no doubt won't go over very well with the bank. There is no way that money order is for real.' But I couldn't come up with anything, so I kept walking and talking and thinking and at no point did it occur to me that I could simply turn to this guy and say, 'I don't believe a word coming out of your mouth, and even though you're obviously a handsome and intelligent man in your early thirties and no doubt could have your pick from all sorts of gainful employment, it's pretty clear that you are trying to con me out of my own hard-earned money.' And the reason I never thought to say this to him wasn't because I was afraid that if I confronted him he'd freak out and kick my ass – I'm a coward, but I'm also foolishly, resplendently proud – it was because I was embarrassed for him. Up until I had agreed to cash the money order, there had been a glimmer of truth, however faint, to his bullshit story, and even though I shouldn't have given it any credence, it was impossible to completely satisfy my doubt so long as he maintained the pretense that he was telling me the truth, and even if he'd come on a little strong, and the desperate tone of his voice suggested that this wasn't the first time he'd been this hard up, his act was somehow convincing. But the moment I agreed to his bogus proposal he was so stunned and full of joy over his dumb luck (i.e. me) that he definitively put to rest even the dimmest possibility that he was telling me the truth, and I could see with agonizing clarity just how fucking stupid I was being. And I was also struck by how pathetic he was. This was my first encounter with a real con man, and instead of the narcissistic calm I'd come to expect from all the crap I watch on TV, he turned out to be a rather ordinary alcoholic, and also an addict (of what, I'm sure I don't know, but something hard) and he was obviously in a chaotic state of total despair. He'd been reduced to cheating naive strangers out of what little money they have. It's shameful to go around conning people like me out of their wages, or inheritance, or stock options, or whatever, and while there may be a few people out there who are actually comfortable with this sort of thing and can hold their heads high and never give a thought to the degradation and corruption of their soul, I'm willing to bet that most people would rather work, even if the work wasn't all that great, maybe even if it was downright shitty, because there is something about ripping people off – even when they can afford it – that offends the sense of fairness that we're either born with or that gets planted in us at an early age. When I looked at his eyes now, eyes that I'd found so wild and mysterious, I saw what was there all along, the blank stare of someone high on hard drugs. To him, I was nothing. The story was nothing. There was only the four hundred dollars. It was possible he wasn't the sort of person who would normally go around cheating people. Maybe in his former life he'd been a minor success, the product of years of patient and unhurried work. He hadn't been ambitious and didn't expect that anything great was in store for him, just a quiet decent life. But a skiing accident, or maybe something even more banal, like a car crash, left him in constant agony and he ended up a slave to his pain meds, lost everything, turned to the harder stuff, and wound up so racked with need that he even tried the old money order con that nobody ever fell for anymore, certainly not with such a strung out and wasted addict like Luke MacDonald. As we made our way to the ATM he insisted on keeping eye contact with me the entire time, which meant that he had to do a mix of side-stepping and light-jogging, at one point even facing me straight on as he jogged backwards. But he wasn't very good at it. He kept bumping into me and tripping us both up, all because he insisted on looking me in the eye while he kept firing questions at me or interjecting with stories of his own childhood, keeping up a staccato pace that was clearly designed to distract me so I wouldn't have an opportunity to back out or to consider more closely everything that he'd said to me and discover some inconsistency or implausibility that I hadn't noticed before, because, as far as he understood, up until now, I wasn't suspicious of him or his story. 'Why, if he had even a shadow of a doubt, would he agree to my proposal?' is what he would think. It's unlikely that I had been his first *mark* that day. It was late and I imagine he'd already been walking the streets for hours, meeting with continual rejection, most *marks* not even letting him get a word in before cutting him off and moving on, while those who listened, even those who listened to the whole story, may have let him down a bit gentler, but until he'd found me he'd been refused by what I'm sure were dozens of people. So he certainly wasn't expecting to be able to get me to listen to him, let alone agree to *cash his money order*, and even once I agreed he must've been skeptical at first, that I was trying to trick him and instead of going to the bank machine I was leading him into a trap. He was an addict after all, and the cruel irony of living in the street, so I've heard, is that they get mugged and ripped off all the time (often by other *street people*). But whatever doubt he may have had about my sincerity disappeared by this point, and he seemed convinced that I actually believed everything he had said. This is why he was so intent on keeping up eye contact, I thought, so he could gauge whether or not I was bullshitting him, or if I was awakening to the fact that he was bullshitting me. By looking into my eyes he believed he could determine if I was lying to him, which is exactly what I believed when I'd still been in doubt over whether the story he was telling was true, and it would be fair to say that in both cases neither of us had any luck with this method. I looked into his eyes – he looked right back at me – and there was nothing I could see that either gave him away or confirmed his story. There was nothing to see, except that his eyes were wild and unblinking, and it was certainly the same with me. I wondered if my eyes looked as wide open and abstracted, like doll's eyes, the realistic kind, where the resemblance to human eyes is uncanny and all the more disturbing for their lifelessness. Or maybe, I thought, they're more like the eyes of someone in the grip of a major stroke, somehow alive but devoid of any trace of intelligence. In short, I wondered if when he looked into my eyes I was as completely gone as he was to me. If someone were to see us right now they wouldn't see things the way I saw them, I thought. They wouldn't see a sad, pathetic, desperate man who was admittedly handsome – though if he wasn't careful he was going to lose his looks through dissipation – they would not see this strung out con man hustling a young, reasonably well-dressed, sympathetic and naive man out of his hard-earned money. No. They would see two wild-eyed men hurrying along the sidewalk and talking loudly and excitedly, and maybe both of them would look sad and desperate so that the passerby thought he was looking at a couple of psychos. But this isn't how things looked to me. Instead, I felt superior to Luke, and while he was trying to keep eye contact with me I was doing the exact opposite, because I was worried that eventually he would realize that I knew he was full of shit and I imagined that he'd be devastated (especially after I'd just got his hopes up) and probably ashamed as well. I hated to see a person lose face, as the Japanese say. In fact, when I learned that the Japanese actually had a word for ritually committing suicide out of shame I instantly became fascinated by Japanese culture. (I've visited Japan twice and I hope to go back again soon.) It may be maudlin, or romantic, or just plain childish to be mortified by another person's humiliation, but I can't help it. When someone is caught in a lie, I'd rather pretend I didn't notice than acknowledge their pathetic attempt to deny a reality that is staring them right in the face. Don't get me wrong, I wasn't willing to hand over four hundred dollars just to avoid an awkward encounter, but so long as I still had a chance, I wanted to come up with something that would allow us both to back off without feeling like idiots. When I am a witness to someone's humiliation it is as though I have been humiliated, just like when a child gets embarrassed during a sex scene from a movie or television show, even if they're alone, because they assume that when their excitement and confusion is this intense *everyone must know*. I assumed that when one person's shameful behaviour is exposed, that the sheer intensity of their humiliation was capable of exposing all of my faults and secrets as well, a sort of shame by association. So when I finally concluded that Luke had been lying to me I reacted as though I had been caught in a lie, as if just by listening to this guy's bullshit story I was equally guilty of deception. On account of some stunted development, an aspect of my personality still stuck in infancy, I can not differentiate between my actions and someone else's. And so maybe he hadn't been that far off when he compared me to Jesus, since I was under the impression that I could take on the sins of the world. What was especially maddening about all of this was that I often ended up feeling guiltier and more embarrassed than the actual guilty party. Everyone feels the sting of their own conscience differently, and what some people consider a grave sin, others aren't bothered by in the least. So when I witnessed what I considered to be shameful and reprehensible behaviour, and responded with a guilty conscience as if I was the one who had behaved shamefully, it was very possible that the person I was feeling guilty on behalf of didn't feel guilty or humiliated at all. I was particularly embarrassed by lying – the greater the lie, the greater the humiliation. In the case of Luke's story, he had lied to me so completely and so thoroughly misrepresented his position that I was *covered with shame*. I just wanted to be rid of him so I could put the whole encounter behind me. I was desperate for him to shut up, to stop adding insult to injury by asking me these ridiculous questions about where I went to school, where my parents were from, what my father did for a living before he retired, and whether or not I had any children. Each question was like a whiplash, a dagger, an icy slap, or a combination of all three (and any other physical assault you can think of), which I could see coming from a great distance but for some fucked up reason was powerless to avoid. It was as though I was being tortured, or had already been tortured, and now my torturer wanted to make small talk, not realizing (or realizing, but not caring) that by acting as though the torture hadn't taken place he was revisiting the whole encounter upon me with a sort of casual cruelty that was literally soul-destroying. 'I can't fucking believe this guy,' I thought. 'Isn't it obvious that I know he's full of shit? Isn't he ashamed to look me in the eye and make small talk when both of us know that all he can think about is the moment that I cash this phony money order and give him four hundred dollars out of my personal banking account? If I were him,' I thought, 'I would apologize and run away and hope that I never saw the person I was trying to rip off (i.e. me) ever again.' My embarrassment had shifted to fury, but I wasn't furious with him for trying to con me out of four hundred dollars – this, I thought, was understandable. The reason that I was so angry with him was because he'd done such a bad job of it. His approach had been so clumsy and the lies he'd told me were so obviously lies that it was impossible for me to believe him. If he'd been more artful, had he taken the time to develop a more plausible story, had he worked on his delivery so it came off smoother and more believable, then I would've been able to fork over the cash with a clean conscience. As it stood, he had forced me into the shameful and humiliating position of either pretending that he had fooled me, giving him four hundred dollars, and returning to my home, to my basement, to contemplate how pathetically I'd reacted to what for most people would be a mildly annoying encounter, or accusing him of lying, calling him out on his bullshit story, and exposing him as a cheat and an utter fraud. 'Why couldn't he have just left me alone,' I said to myself, 'instead of more or less forcing me to expose him, and myself, to unbearable shame?' In short, I was enraged by what I perceived to be an imposition. He was obliging me to share in his degradation, which in my opinion, was even worse than cheating me out of four hundred dollars, and no matter what I did (give him the money or refuse to give him the money) there was no way I could avoid the fact that this good-looking and, by my estimation, intelligent stranger had sunk so low that he'd been reduced to approaching guys like me on the street and screwing them out of their money. If he'd been more resourceful then he could've come up with a story that might have flattered my self-regard, while preserving the illusion of his own good character. 'But this idiot,' I thought, 'this *crackhead*, has made the whole situation so glaringly apparent, that there's no way to get out of it without feeling like a complete piece of shit. The genie is out of the bottle. Pandora is out of her box.' Blah blah blah. 'Just go away,' I thought. 'Leave me alone. Disappear.' But it was evident that he had no intention of leaving now that I had agreed to cash his fraudulent money order. 'There's no way I'm going through with this. There's no way I'm giving this guy four hundred dollars,' I thought, and just as I was thinking this we arrived at the bank machine and he held the door to the vestibule for me with the exaggerated manners of an erstwhile gentleman down on his luck. And even as I was putting my card in the bank machine and entering my PIN, I was still under the impression that something would come to me, some excuse that would get me out of this infuriating and embarrassing situation. He was standing right behind me and by now he'd grown so eager and excited that he'd lost all control of himself. He started telling me what to do, as if he wasn't a con man anymore and was actually holding me up at knife-point. 'Deposit,' he said. 'It's just like a regular deposit. Put it in this envelope,' he said, and he reached across me to get an envelope from the slot, but I pushed his hand away as if he'd triggered a reflex, or maybe I had reached my limit – whatever the reason for it, the moment his hand snaked in front of me (which also meant he had to lean in so that his mouth was only a few centimetres away from my ear), I smacked it away so quickly and forcefully that I surprised myself, and him, since my reaction seemed to come from nowhere. Even though I was choking with rage over the way he was essentially mugging me, I hadn't been worried that I was going to snap and lash out at him like that. I assumed that the most I would do was make an irritated remark, since I knew myself well enough to know that I would avoid a physical confrontation at any cost, or at least, in this case, I was willing to give a stranger four hundred dollars in order to avoid not only a physical confrontation, but also an emotional one. My theory is that it was at this point – when he leaned in and reached in front of me to grab an envelope – that I realized I was going to give him the money. From the moment he had approached me until the moment I smacked his hand away there had never been a moment when I wasn't going to give him the money. 'All that crap about whether he was telling the truth or not was complete bullshit,' I thought. 'You (i.e. me) were always going to give him the four hundred dollars.' Just like when I went down into the basement with the intention of working on my life's work, and ended up doing everything except what I had intended to do, it was clear that I had known what was going to happen all along, and instead of just admitting this to myself I had to enact an elaborate scenario that dramatized all the steps of making a choice, in order to justify the choice that I had already made. One of the reasons (I suspect) that I decided at a very early age to devote myself to a goal that I would most likely never achieve, but that required *blind devotion*, unwavering commitment, and spending what seemed like every moment of my waking life at work or planning to work, or thinking about what I would do next time I sat down to work, was that by making this choice I was absolving myself of ever having to make a choice again. Ever since that one big choice there have been nothing but *sub-choices* or *leftover choices*, since all I had to decide was how they either advanced or impeded the realization of my final goal (my life's work), which technically isn't a decision so much as it is the continued administration of the one true initial choice. There was no confusion for me when I woke up each day over how I should spend my time – my *free time*, that is – since I knew that all my free time should be spent in pursuit of my goal, and every aspect of my life – what I ate, when I slept, how I dressed – was decided based on what I thought would help in realizing my life's work. Now, as I've already explained, I don't know where this initial decision came from to devote my life to a goal that very few people ever attain (and even if they do attain this goal, it may not happen in their lifetime, and if it does happen in their lifetime they may not even realize that it happened, and even if it does happen in their lifetime and they realize it happened, it's more than likely that nobody else will realize that it happened, or people may deny it or claim that even though it may seem like it happened, it in fact didn't happen at all, but no matter what happens, the only way to have a hope in hell of attaining this lofty unattainable goal in the first place is to stick to your guns, never give up, even when it seems like there's no chance, that you're a lost cause, when everyone is telling you to let it go, that there's no shame in defeat, that you gave it your best, that to keep working would be stupid, self-destructive, and just plain selfish, no matter what anybody says or what you think or how you feel, there's no turning back, so even when I was wasting my time down in the basement, and possibly sabotaging the time I'd already spent on my life's work by going over everything that I had already done, I was still convinced that all of this was necessary and was part of the process of reaching an unattainable goal) but my point is simply that while many people believe that it takes an incredible amount of strength, will, determination, and even courage to spend one's life in pursuit of a grandly elusive goal, I would suggest that the truth is much less flattering. The truth is that when someone makes a choice to devote themselves to their life's work they are also choosing to never have to bother with concepts like strength or will or courage for the remainder of their days. And I'm sure that the ultimate reason behind my mindless rage over this encounter was because the stranger was forcing a decision on me that I didn't want to make. Had it only been a matter of deciding whether he was telling the truth or not, there might not have been much of a decision to make in the first place, but since I knew he was lying it was clear that what I was choosing between was whether I wanted to confront him or just give him the money and avoid a confrontation. And, as I said, once this choice became apparent it occurred to me that I had known he was lying all along and that I had only pretended otherwise because I'd already decided to give him the money. Or was there another reason I went along with the con, a behavioural reflex or temporary insanity? When he started more or less mugging me at the bank machine all of what I've just explained became *painfully obvious* to me. I was sick of the whole thing and wanted it to be over with as soon as possible, so after I'd knocked his hand away I deposited the money order and withdrew four hundred and handed it over . . . or did he snatch it out of my hands? . . . My memory is fuzzy on that point. . . . When he started to thank me I cut him off and told him that he'd already thanked me and he didn't need to keep on thanking me. Once was enough. 'Besides,' I said, 'I just made a hundred bucks.'

MARY

They don't tell you about this when you're young, or, if they did, I wasn't paying attention. For some reason we treat it like it's a big secret. I mean, I'd heard about it, I knew it was a *thing*, but nobody *really* talked about it. And nobody talks about it now either, including me. I talk about it with James, of course, but that doesn't count. We talk about everything, or at least as much as a married couple can manage. Obviously there's stuff you shouldn't say, but sometimes I end up saying it anyway. It's weird. It's like I forget who I'm talking to. No, it's more like I think I'm talking to a different James instead of the one that I'm actually talking to and I end up saying things to the imaginary 'James' that the actual James probably shouldn't hear. I think he can take it, but then I realize that it doesn't matter whether he can take it or not, there are some things, big surprise, that you just shouldn't say out loud. But this isn't one of those things. What's worse is that not only does nobody talk about it, but what little they do say is misleading, so you end up feeling like a freak if your experience doesn't match up with that of these good-intentioned people. Growing up, they lead you to believe that getting pregnant is as easy as catching a fucking cold. In grade nine, a girl in my class got pregnant, and the way everyone talked about her made it seem like if you had sex there was a ninety-nine percent chance you were going to have a baby. It didn't matter if you used condoms because there were all sorts of stories about people who went to drugstores and poked holes in them, or they broke, or they came off while you were doing it, or you put it on wrong in the first place. The pill was supposed to work, but then somebody would tell you about how their cousin was on the pill, and used a condom, and only had sex once, and she got pregnant. For obvious reasons they kept us in the dark. They didn't tell us that you could be perfectly healthy, have sex with a perfectly healthy guy, that he could come inside of you while you were in the fertile period of your cycle, and that despite all of this (despite doing exactly what you were supposed to do in order to get pregnant) nothing would happen. Obviously none of this bothered me when I wasn't trying to get pregnant – I just assumed that I didn't get pregnant because I was doing everything right. By that I mean that I was doing everything I needed to be doing in order *not* to get pregnant. But maybe it had nothing to do with what I was doing. Maybe I didn't get pregnant back then because I couldn't. It's possible I didn't even have to use birth control – that if I stopped using the pill, condoms, sponges, diaphragms, and all that other crap, that nothing would've happened anyway. I had been brainwashed into thinking that having sex and not getting pregnant was so rare you had a better chance of getting hit by lightning, twice, while simultaneously winning the lottery. They didn't tell us the truth – that it was possible to have unprotected sex again and again without getting pregnant. They never prepared me for this and so when it happened to me it took a few months before I could recognize what was going on. When we decided to *pull the goalie* and started actually trying to get pregnant we expected that it would happen right away. So when it didn't happen we automatically assumed that we were doing something wrong. 'Are you sure that you came inside me?' I would ask after getting my period, and James always answered back with the same irritated tone that yes, he was *very sure*. Even though I knew he was telling me the truth – after all I had felt him come, and I could feel it running out of me – I still thought that maybe he was mistaken, that he'd thought he'd come inside when he'd actually pulled out at the last second. Or maybe, I thought, he did come inside but it hadn't been deep enough. Maybe, even though it felt like he was coming in me, his dick was barely inside me, and this was why it didn't work. But after we'd been trying for a couple months I started to think that something else was wrong. I'd read a ton of stuff online about the ovulation cycle and was pretty sure that we were having sex during my fertile period. I used those strips that tell you when you're ovulating, and I also learned how to check my cervical mucus for signs that the egg had dropped. I got a basal thermometer and started tracking my temperature. After months of doing all this crap and still not getting pregnant I started to worry that I was doing it all wrong. 'Maybe the strips are defective,' I thought. 'Maybe I'm not reading the thermometer correctly, or maybe it's broken.' The whole cervical mucus thing was particularly frustrating because the description of what I should be looking for ('clear and stretchy – similar to the consistency of egg whites') seemed to leave so much open to interpretation that I could never be sure of what I had going on. I couldn't trust anything. So the only way to be sure that we were having sex during my fertile period was to start having sex every day. And so here was another thing they don't tell you about when you're young. The way that everyone talks about sex, the way it's represented on TV and in movies and books and music, leads you to believe that there's nothing better than sex, and that getting to have sex every day would be like a dream come true. But anybody who *actually* has sex knows that this is complete horseshit. Don't get me wrong, I like having sex as much as the next gal, though I'm definitely more into quality than quantity. Even if James and I were five years younger, even if we'd just

GIVING UP

met and everything was new and exciting, I would still consider having sex every day to be more of a curse than a blessing. But after five years together I'm sure I don't have to explain why this is causing us a shitload of problems. Based on what has turned out to be a false assumption (that having sex during my fertile period would lead to pregnancy) I had reached two equally false conclusions (that we weren't doing it right, *and* that we weren't doing it at the right times) and as a result of these two false conclusions we started having sex every day. This was the only way we could be one hundred percent sure that we weren't leaving anything to chance. James referred to this strategy as *blitzkrieging the womb*, and it was obvious by the way he said it that he didn't think it was going to work. But since he didn't have any other ideas, and since what we'd been doing wasn't working, he conceded that I was right, it was *the only way to be sure*. The moment my period stopped we started having sex, and we didn't stop having sex until my period started again. It's a cliché that married couples rarely have sex, and that when they do it's a joyless exercise, and there's a related cliché that when a married couple is trying to get pregnant the sex they are having is the most pragmatic and joyless of all. And the cliché about clichés – that they are clichés for a reason, because they are actually true – could probably be applied to our situation. I'm not saying that the sex was awful. Quite the opposite, actually. Since we were having so much sex we definitely improved over time, to the point where we could pull the whole thing off in under five minutes. And even though we were having sex all the time we didn't fall back on routine. We made a huge effort to keep things fresh so that the whole thing wouldn't turn into something unpleasant that we didn't look forward to, or that we might try to avoid. In the end though, all that came from this was that it made us feel more alone, more lost. James was very aware of how anxious I was that there might be something wrong with me and that this was the reason I couldn't get pregnant (and not because we weren't doing it right) and he did everything he could to be considerate while we were having sex. He kept things light and tried to distract me by focusing my attention on the nuts and bolts of what we were doing, and it was actually very sweet, but even though he was so attentive and caring he ended up coming off as needy, and instead of creating an intimate mood it could get pretty tense. For my part I tried to keep the sex low-impact, because I was self-conscious of how our sex schedule conflicted with his nightly routine of spending hours and hours doing God knows what down in the basement. I picked times when he took one of his breaks from his work, so he wouldn't see it as an interruption or a distraction, and might even look forward to it as a way of unwinding. And while we were having sex I also did my best to keep it light, and tried to turn him on by doing things that weren't really how I got off but that I knew he liked. If he couldn't get it up I always did my best to reassure him and told him that we could try later, and sometimes we would. In a way, our sex life had never been as good as it was when we were trying to get pregnant. We'd never been so considerate and kind and attentive and dear to each other, but none of that ultimately mattered because our daily regimen of sex was putting incredible pressure on our relationship. It didn't matter what we did, we couldn't ignore the fact that if we weren't trying to get pregnant we wouldn't be having sex on a daily basis. Even though it was really nice in a lot of ways and brought us closer together and all that, there was no denying that we were both in despair over having to fake it like this. It wasn't because of anything that happened while we were having sex, just that we didn't have a choice in the matter. We *had* to have sex every day to ensure that we were doing everything possible to get pregnant. To be blunt, if we didn't cover every base then we couldn't forgive ourselves once my cycle was over and it was apparent that, yet again, I didn't get pregnant. What made everything worse – what made the whole routine so demoralizing and even depressing – was that even though both of us tried to keep a positive outlook and hope that all this sex would result in me getting pregnant, we both suspected there was something permanently wrong that no amount of sex would be able to cure. I don't remember exactly when I noticed this was the case, but I think it would be fair to say that after six months of this daily sex routine both us *knew* nothing would come of it. Every month we would have sex every day but nothing ever happened. I would eventually start feeling all the symptoms that signalled I was going to get my period soon, and then it would come, and we would start all over again. This drained the whole thing of the pleasure we should've been experiencing. We knew we were going to have to keep trying, and that it didn't matter what we did to make sure our daily routine didn't become a chore that eroded the bonds of our love and affection – this erosion was inevitable. So even if the sex was good – which it often was – mutual resentment started to creep in, and every night we looked forward to our sex routine with dread. Since we both knew that this was possibly going to destroy our relationship we started to talk about going to the doctor. If we could confirm that there was nothing wrong with us (biologically that is) then we'd be able to maintain our optimism because we could be sure that even though we were having a hard time, our routine would eventually pay off. 'If I just knew that at the end of all this I was going to get pregnant,' I'd say to James, 'then I'd be able to handle anything.' If the sex wasn't good, if James couldn't get it up, or got it up but couldn't keep it up, or if he could only keep it up by getting all distant and just pounding away, obviously fantasizing about someone else, then I would try to reassure myself by dreaming about when I would finally get *pregnant*, but at some point our mutual despair just became too strong, it was impossible to fake it like we'd been doing for the first six months, and I stopped trying to reassure myself because I had pretty much lost all hope that it was ever going to work. 'At the end of it all,' I thought, 'we will be exactly where we were at the start.' 'We just need to confirm whether or not something is wrong,' James would say, once it became obvious after more than a year that we were starting to despair. 'Even if it turns out that something *is* wrong, at least we'll know what we're dealing with.' Once we finished having sex, once we had tenderly and considerately seen to each other's sexual needs, we

GIVING UP

would lie next to each other and I would immediately sink into despairing thoughts about how, even though we were doing everything right, the chance that this most recent sexual encounter would result in pregnancy was highly unlikely. (And yet, this time had as much of a chance of being *the time* as any other time we had sex. So it was hard not to get my hopes up.) I'm sure he was having the same thoughts, and if we had admitted to each other that we were sinking into despair then we might have been able to comfort one another, but instead we kept it all hidden from each other and pretended that we were feeling optimistic. Never admitting what we were really feeling eventually led to resentment, because even though we both pretended that we were optimistic, it was obvious we knew that we were pretending. If we'd just been honest about how we were really feeling then we might have been able to avoid these feelings of resentment. So we agreed to go to a doctor, basically to reassure each other, since we're apparently incapable of reassuring each other on our own. 'At least this way we can be sure,' James said, 'that there's nothing wrong with us.' Our daily routine, our monthly routine (and now *yearly* routine) had become so depressing that the only way we could keep from *sinking into total despair* was to get medical confirmation of some *biological* explanation for why we were having trouble getting pregnant. 'This way,' James said, 'we'll be able to relax, because at least we'll have a better idea of what the problem is.' James always talks as though we are in this together, that this is just as difficult for him as it is for me, which, no matter how hard I try not to let it, deeply offends me. He claims to want a child just as much as I do, but we both know that this is total garbage. There's no way that he wants a child even a fraction as much as I do. There's no way he *could* want a child the way I do. Full disclosure: if I hadn't come to James and told him how much I wanted to start a family together ('more than anything') then it's more than likely he would have been happy to wait for years before he brought it up. Knowing him, he'd leave it until I was way past menopause and then act all surprised, like 'Really? I guess I never thought about it that way.' There's no way for me to prove it, but I'm almost one hundred percent sure that there's a significant part of him that would've been happy to keep doing what he was doing indefinitely. Nothing ever changing. I've always been the one to suggest that we take the next step. I'm the one who wants our relationship to progress, while James, from what I can tell, is determined to maintain stasis. It was me, not James, who suggested that we move in together after we had been dating (exclusively) for more than two years. And I was the one, after we had been living together as common-law for at least five years, who proposed that we finally make it official and get married, not in a religious ceremony, but in a civil ceremony, by a justice of the peace. And once we got married I was the one who gave the ultimatum that within a year I wanted to be *with child*. So when James insisted that this was just as important for him as it was for me I found it hard not to call him out on that. Not that he didn't want children – I'm sure that in an abstract, high-minded sort of way he did – but I knew that if I gave any indication that I didn't believe he wanted a child as much as I did he would freak out. The handful of occasions that I haven't been able to hide how I really feel on this subject have resulted in huge, multi-day arguments. He literally can't stand knowing that I don't believe him, even though he doesn't even bother concealing the fact that he doesn't actually believe himself. This is what I can't stand. If he admitted that he didn't want a child as much as I did I wouldn't be bothered at all. But since he insists that we both want a child with the same level of need and longing and urgency, and since he insists on this with such infuriating stubbornness, sometimes, when we are talking about getting pregnant (which is basically the only thing we talk about these days), I feel like I am losing my mind. Like I am actually losing the ability to distinguish between reality and fantasy. 'Which is why we need to see a specialist,' James says, 'so that we can stop living in limbo.' (One time, he said 'hell' instead of 'limbo.') 'That way, even if it's bad news, we'll know what we're dealing with.' James wanted to stop 'dealing in conjecture' and find out 'what the real issue is.' 'We don't have to live in ignorance like this,' he said to me, as if I was an idiot. 'There's all sorts of resources available to people like us. What's the point of living in the twenty-first century, in one of the richest countries in the world, in one of the most privileged socio-economic classes within this country, with some of the most talented and educated specialists in the entire profession, and some of the most advanced technology known to *man*, if we aren't going to take advantage of our advantages?' When he gets worked up like this, when he starts dropping terms like 'socio-economic,' and saying things like 'take advantage of our advantages,' it's only a matter of time before he completely freaks out. Usually I try to hide what I'm really thinking and just agree with everything he says, although it's important that I agree enthusiastically, so that he thinks I don't just agree with him, but that he is actually explaining my own thoughts to me so that I can understand them more fully than if I'd been left to contemplate them on my own. Sometimes I slip up, maybe out of irritation, but most likely from boredom, and I end up saying the very thing that will make him hysterical. Instead of telling him the real reason I'm reluctant to go see a specialist, I make something up based on opinions and beliefs I don't possess but that I know from experience will drive him into an exasperated rage. 'Nothing is one hundred percent, James,' is what I say. 'All those over-educated doctors and their million-dollar machines still manage to get it wrong all the time. And even if they aren't wrong, they probably won't be able to tell us what we want to know. You haven't read as much about this as I have,' I say, knowing full well that it's things like this that make him almost speechless with anger. 'All they can tell you is that there's nothing wrong. That's the best we can hope for. But even when there's nothing wrong people still end up not being able to have children. There's no medical explanation. One in ten women who can't conceive have no idea what's wrong with them. It just doesn't work. So I know you think that we're going to get some sort of diagnosis or something like that, but that's not really how it works. It's true,' I say, 'that sometimes they can tell you if something is wrong, like if you have a *low sperm count*, or if they find *cysts in my uterus* or something like that. But a lot of the time they don't find anything. Most of the time they can't even tell you what's wrong.' Even though this was all true, I knew that James would disagree. I'll admit that there was a part of me that wanted to provoke him, to piss him off, but once I had finished I realized that he was going to argue with me, and I regretted saying what I'd said, because while I had accomplished my goal of enraging James, I knew that whatever he was going to say was going to be extremely upsetting for me, and that without intending to, I had brought on the exact scenario I'd been desperate to avoid. The thing that pissed me off so much was that James was willing to argue with me even when he had no idea what he was talking about. I had just stated some inarguable facts about what we could expect when we went in for testing. These facts came from the medical literature I'd been reading about pregnancy, as well as from my friends who had *first-hand experience* due to their own problems with getting pregnant. But just because he felt that what I had said was incorrect, even though he had nothing to base this feeling on, he had no problem telling me that 'it might be a little more complex than that.' 'Don't get me wrong,' he said, aware that he was about to provoke a full-on fight, 'I know that you've read way more about this than I have, but from what I understand it's a little less mysterious than that.' While James was explaining conception to me my mind started to drift, and somehow I ended up at the memory of an episode of *Cheers* I saw only once when I was in junior high. In the episode, Sam and Kirstie Alley were trying to have a baby together, and there must've been a problem with Sam's sperm because Kirstie Alley kept on nagging him about wearing refrigerated underwear and other things that are supposed to help with *motility*. This was when I first learned that people had to *try* to get pregnant, and that it wasn't easy, that they had to try all the time, and that nothing may come of it. No baby. So I guess what I said earlier about being completely misled about the problems that women have with getting pregnant wasn't entirely accurate. My teachers, my parents, my aunts and uncles, my friends, my friends' parents – literally everyone I knew never – said a thing, nothing in school or in anything I read ever referred to it, but on TV I found out that people could have sex – constantly – and never get pregnant. I'm not talking about being barren. I'm not referring to the movies of the week that dealt with women who had to adopt babies, or steal them, or have them implanted in their uteruses, or in the uterus of someone else, in order to enjoy the privilege of being a mother. A barren woman is someone who knows that they can never get pregnant – maybe they've had their ovaries removed, or they had some weird infection that fucked with their tubes – whereas someone who is infertile is perfectly capable of getting pregnant, but for whatever reason it doesn't work for them. So I'm not thinking about the sweet middle-aged women in movies or sitcoms or shitty novels, who, despite the fact that they're always ridiculously likeable, have a really sad and lonely thing going on, and who you eventually find out can't 'conceive' or 'bear children,' usually because of something really traumatic (and lurid and incestuous, or luridly incestuous, from their past), and even though back then I couldn't appreciate what a unique service *Cheers* provided for everyone going through the same thing, I'm glad to know that at least one TV show was doing the right thing. Of course now that I'm going through it there's no end to the amount of shit you can find online. James is right when he says I know a lot more about it than he does, I do, but this doesn't stop him from trying to tell me about it. 'They have all sorts of tests they can do now,' he said, 'and usually they can tell you if – you know – something is wrong or not. And if there is then . . . well . . . you know . . . there's stuff they can do sometimes to fix it.' (What he didn't say was that if they don't find anything, and there's nothing wrong with me, then there's basically nothing they can do.) 'This happens all the time,' he said. 'I know you've read more and I'm not arguing that. I'm just saying that there's other stories out there. . . . I've met people, and everyone has a story like this. If it's not about them, then it's someone they know,' he said earlier this evening from his usual perch at the foot of the bed, while I'd taken shelter under the covers. We had just tried to have sex but he couldn't get it up and I wasn't up for going through the routine we had for this scenario. It requires a lot of effort and patience on my part, something that usually doesn't bother me (it's not all that different from some kind of boring but physically invigorating chore, like landscaping or snow-shovelling) but since on this occasion I could see that he took it for granted and expected me to go through this routine, I got annoyed. It was annoying, the way he expected me to go along with his little fantasies, and all at once I decided that there was no way I was going to be able to go through the motions this time. James basically expects me to do all the work. I'm the one that has to make it happen. There is really no telling what his dick is going to do. He might go on a streak for months, only to slip into a funk that lasts twice as long. When he gets like this, he speaks about his dick as if it's out of his control, like some sort of wild beast or a force of nature. According to him, the only way to get it to work again was if I pretended that there was nothing wrong. 'Just keep doing what you're doing,' he said, ignoring the fact that it was physically impossible for me to keep doing what I was doing. So eventually I gave up and this led to an argument. So ... fucking ... predictable. The stupid thing about this specific argument we had on the night of the cat incident was that I had taken up the exact opposite side than the one I was actually on. It was me, not James, who first suggested that we go see a fertility doctor. I was the one who suggested that we should get tested. But the reason I was taking the other side and pretending that I wasn't entirely behind the plan of making an appointment with a fertility doctor for this month was that I could tell that James believed that if there was a problem, it didn't have anything to do with him. He was obsessed with the idea of seeing a fertility doctor because, instead of seeing our problem as something that we should go through together, like a quest, he saw the whole thing as a kind of game that we were playing against each other, and I could tell that he thought he was winning. When he said that he 'just wanted to do it sooner, rather than later,' he was, as he saw it, calling my bluff. And instead of confronting him head-on by telling him that I had already looked into it and made an appointment for next week (all true), I messed around with him for a bit. Whenever he gets worked up he starts talking a lot of garbage, like complete nonsense, so it's easy to trip him up. He isn't really paying attention to the words coming out of his mouth. It's not like I made a conscious decision to piss him off, but in retrospect I'll admit that this was what I was doing. But now that I'm telling this I feel like I'm painting an ugly picture of our relationship. The majority of the time we're great. There is so much I'm leaving out, all the ways that we love each other and the daily kindnesses, the sacrifices, all that. But that's not really the story I'm telling because this isn't really about our relationship at all, this is just about what happened with the cat. So it's a coincidence that on the night of the cat incident we happened to be having a fight, that's why I'm focussing so much on all of this, and not because I think we have a bad relationship. So my point is just that James has been in a slump. The only time he goes down to the basement anymore is when we get in a fight, and the only time he leaves the apartment (and doesn't come back for hours) is when he's been down in the basement, working on something that he's been saying for years is 'almost complete'. Which, as I said, doesn't really bother me, but definitely bothers him. That's the whole point to telling all of this. To give some context for how I was feeling that night. Whenever we fight I always get really tired afterwards. And we'd been fighting so much that week that I was in a sort of waking coma. We went from being really tender and sweet one moment, to saying the most bitterly hateful things the next. No matter how many times we fight I can never get used to how we change so completely. It's hard to describe. I invariably end up using the same clichéd expressions you hear all the time. 'It was like he was a different person,' or 'We were looking at each other like complete strangers.' But when I try to break down the feeling into the most simple components I have to admit that it's actually not all that complicated. When we are being kind to each other, when we are being patient, sweet, and understanding, it feels as though this is the way it always is, as if this is the only reality that exists, and even though I know that we fight all the time, the memory of these fights is completely unreal, like I'm remembering a dream, and somehow I end up believing that even though we fight a lot, it doesn't really matter, because that's not *who we really are*. When we do get into a fight, however, I feel the exact opposite way. It's as if all that tenderness and patience is an act, that the only thing we ever really do is fight, and that even when we're not fighting, all we're doing is biding our time until the next confrontation. And of course, since we can shift so quickly from cuddling on the couch to screaming in each other's faces, I end up feeling like I'm losing my grip on reality. Which, in a way, I am. The analogy I always use is that it feels like I'm a nun who keeps losing her faith and then finding it again, on a daily basis. Because, just like a nun, when I lose my faith, I lose it completely. When we argue I basically start mentally packing my bags. There is no hope for us. There never was. We were just going through the motions. We were never really in love. When we go into that hole, when it goes dark between us, it feels as though even in the most recent past, when we were being loving with one another, that I never really felt the way that I thought I felt towards James. I just wanted to believe that I felt that way, I thought. But then, once we made up, I realized the only real thing I have in my life, the only thing I could believe in, the only person I could count on, was James. 'You're too much of an idealist,' he says. 'How much of an idealist is the right amount?' is what I say. He's into nuance, the grey area. I'm more of a black and whiter, myself. I know that the world is really complex and that nothing is ever one hundred percent, that you can't ever really know the truth about anything and all that crap, but that's not really how it feels. For me, there's not a whole lot of complexity. There's zero nuance. The feeling I have pretty much all the time is that the truth is staring me directly in the face, like right up in my face, breathing all over me and looking deep into my eyes, and just like in real life, if someone is standing that close with their face pressed up against your face so that your noses are touching, looking you right in the eye, it's only natural to look away. It's exhausting to maintain eye contact with someone else, especially if they initiate the eye contact, all you can do is stare back at them and try to keep a straight face that denies them access, as you're basically held hostage by their stare, or you can give in and let them see whatever it is they think they can see by staring for so long. Either way, most of the time, if you're like me, you pretend that you don't notice them staring, and act as if you're lost in thought, even though you're not really acting at all. What you're actually doing by avoiding eye contact is saying to the person staring at you that no matter how penetrating and persuasive their gaze may be, you will never acknowledge the look they are giving you, and by refusing to make eye contact you are saying to the person looking at you that whatever it is they think they see, they aren't really seeing it, that whatever they think they know, or what they think they've just found out, they don't really know, and they haven't found out. By avoiding eye contact you are saying, 'You may think you can see something, but it's not really there. It doesn't exist for me.' When the truth is staring me right in the face, I instinctually look away, but just like when somebody is staring at me, I can feel it no matter what I do. It takes way more energy to constantly look things in the eye. Looking away gives me a bit of control over what I consider to be a pretty intense and unrelenting situation, even though I know this is actually the dictionary definition of sticking your head in the sand. What can I say? Maybe there are advantages to sticking your head in the sand. What's the value in seeing things coming? When a nurse is giving you a shot they tell you to look away because if you can't see what's happening then you may not even notice the pain caused by the needle, but if you insist on watching you end up anticipating the pain, you imagine the needle entering your arm and piercing the fat and muscle, and the anticipation of what's about to happen is worse than the needle itself, or, to put it another way, if you know what's going to happen then everything gets worse. Which is why, when a painful truth is staring me right in the face, I prefer to look away. Even though it felt like something was wrong and that the reason I couldn't get pregnant was that I was barren or James was shooting blanks, everyone I talked to all said the same thing – they knew someone who took a year, two years, three years, somebody else had a cousin who had completely given up and then got pregnant while she was in China to pick up her adopted baby. 'How long have you been trying?' they ask, and when I tell them that it's been more than a year, they wave me off and tell me that it's completely normal at my age to initially have problems getting pregnant. Despite all these anecdotes and words of encouragement I know for a fact that something is wrong. How do I know? Because I know. Because it's staring me right in the face. It should've been as obvious to me then as it's obvious to me now. Going to the doctor to have all these tests done basically allows me to confirm what I already know, because I can *feel* that something is wrong. Even though there was no reason for me to suspect I would be one of the six percent of women that can't have children, or that I might marry someone who falls into the percentage of men that for whatever reason can't make it work, I should've at least considered the possibility when I started thinking about having a baby that it might never happen for me. By now, all of my friends have kids. A lot of them are working on their second. If you were to look at a picture of me and my friends back when we were young, there wouldn't have been anything to tell us apart. We all looked the same, wore the same clothes, did our hair the same way, made the same faces, and struck the same poses. (It's kind of ironic that at precisely the age we think we are most ourselves, or that we are somehow unique and original, we are actually the *least like ourselves* and completely *unoriginal*.) I know it's crazy, but I feel like you can tell somehow, like you can see all my friends' future children crowding the frame like a bunch of unborn ghosts, while surrounding me you might see an empty aura, like a sad little halo, or something like that. I'm not religious. I don't believe we were put on this planet for a reason, or that something happens or doesn't happen for a reason. There's no plan for us. No higher power is watching over us. There's no such thing as fate. I know all of this. But when I think of everything that has happened over the past couple of years, and all that is still happening, I can't shake the feeling that I'm being tested by *something*. It's like everything is building up to a climax, and if I can just hang on and be patient then it'll all work out somehow. Sometimes, even though I know it's a complete fantasy, this theory is the only one that makes any sense. Otherwise, I think, everything that has happened to me and the problems I'm having with getting pregnant are just part of a chaotic swirl and don't mean anything at all and the reason I can't get pregnant is a total fluke and not because of anything wrong with me or James. When I look at these pictures of me and my friends when we were young it's hard not to project what I know now onto who we were back then, and when I look at all the photos they post online now, it's like I'm looking at the fulfillment of a prophesy that was made back when all my old high school photos were taken. On the night of the cat incident this is what I was doing – I was going down the social networking rabbit hole. When James left for one of his 'breaks' I'd been writing an email to my sister about everything that was going on and how I was feeling. But as soon as I took a pause from my email, I decided to check Facebook. Like most people, I spend an hour or two every day torturing myself by going online and indulging in the most ridiculous shit. I tell myself that I'm keeping up to date on the lives of my friends, that I'm maintaining my social life by interacting through short public messages with the handful of my friends who actually bother to maintain an *online presence*. I tell myself that – as I scan hundreds of pictures of my friends – I am just doing what everyone else is doing and that keeping up this loose network of friends, family, and acquaintances, despite my deep ambivalence, is an essential part of being a functioning member of society. I want to emphasize that I'm sure a lot of people have a way better experience with Facebook than I do. It's more than possible that the problems I have with social networks are actually just my own problems, or that the problems I have with Facebook are simply an extension of the problems I have with myself. But even if that is true, it hardly helps me with the feeling I get after I spend any amount of time online. As I said, it starts out innocently enough. I might go online to do some banking or to check the movie times, but within a few clicks I end up on Facebook. I don't think about it, it just happens, and once I'm on Facebook I immediately start telling myself I should get off. I know what being on Facebook does to me, and as soon as I realize what I've done I tell myself that nothing good is going to come of looking at my friends' photos. Then I feel like an asshole because I can't just enjoy looking at pictures of my friends on vacation, or with their children, or read about their great careers or creative projects, without experiencing powerful feelings of envy, and for some reason, anger, and a whole lot of other feelings I can't even name. What kind of person am I that I can't just be excited and supportive of my friends, and be happy for them when it looks like everything is going their way? Why do I resent the way they tell me about the joy and successes in their lives? Would I really appreciate it if they started talking about their failures, or wouldn't I just find some twisted way to resent that too, and somehow, through some ridiculous logic, get jealous over their suffering, as if it was another thing they had that I wanted? At the very least I would probably think they were overreacting, or they were too full of self-pity to notice their problems weren't really problems at all, just the cost of doing business out there in the real world. By using a combination of these arguments, and others like them, I end up staying on Facebook as a sort of challenge, daring myself to go on there and feel nothing but good will and happiness for my friends and family, but this doesn't stop me from continuing to repeat to myself the entire time I'm on Facebook that I'll get off after I look at one more picture, or one more post, or link. I think, 'After this album from Veronica's European vacation I will close down Facebook and go do something more productive,' but of course as soon as I finish looking at those photos I immediately go to another friend's profile to see if they've posted any new pictures. Each picture feels like an insult. I open up a picture of my friends having a picnic in a park to celebrate their daughter's second birthday and it's as if the people in the picture collectively reached out and slapped me right in the face as hard as they could. My friend is smiling into the camera as she helps her daughter open a birthday gift but she might as well be spitting in my face. Even though what I'm looking at is just one picture out of thousands, a completely normal and clichéd snapshot of one of the ordinary milestones that litter my friends' lives, that increasingly clog up all of our lives so that it feels like they're made up entirely of milestones, I feel as though I have been personally insulted by this image. They must realize, I think, as I scroll through reams of snapshots, how painful it is for someone like me to see them enjoying a life that I'll never know. There's no excuse for this kind of shameless showing-off. They post all these pictures under the pretense of sharing these moments with their *online community* but all they're really doing is putting themselves on display. There are pictures of them on sailboats, or on the summit of a South American mountain, or they're laughing their asses off at a wedding, or dancing up a storm at an *exclusive after-party*, but even though the subject of these pictures is constantly changing, the message is always the same. *Look at me.* In short, these pictures are telling us that our friends' lives are orgies of fulfillment, an unending stream of satisfying moments spent with friends and family in exotic and beautiful locations. Even though I know that it's all an act, that what they're actually doing is covering up for all the time they spend alone, or surrounded by strangers, or people they don't like at all and who don't like them, wasting away years of our lives in their sad little offices, eating their sad little lunches, or hiding away in their cramped apartments and run-down houses, even though it's obvious that they're trying to put out a different image of their lives, there's something about these photos that is so convincing that I can't help but think that maybe their lives really are as fulfilling as these photos seem to suggest. Maybe, when I'm staring at the photo of my friend with her husband and two kids in some picturesque vista, posing at the edge of a cliff somewhere in Ireland, overlooking a magnificent stretch of bright blue ocean, I'm not looking at a carefully composed lie, but the gospel truth. It's nearly impossible to distinguish between what is actually happening and what we want each other to think is happening. I've become so obsessed with trying to determine what's going on in these pictures that I end up analyzing them with the same focus and attention to detail that an art expert would use with a painting they've been asked to authenticate. The problem with this is that Facebook photos aren't masterpieces. With art, an expert can draw on their vast knowledge of painting technique and themes, history, and biography – even biology and chemistry – they can look at a picture until they lose themselves in the infinite possibilities of interpretation, and they can try to determine what the artist intended, and whether they succeeded, and, if they didn't succeed, why not. But a Facebook photo isn't really meant to be analyzed, that's why you end up scrolling through a bunch at a time, because on their own there's not really much to look at, it's more about getting information than anything else. Whenever I go to a gallery, which isn't very often, I always leave with a sense of exhilaration, a sense of possibility, a feeling that the world which often seems so limited is actually so full that it's literally swelling. But every time I spend an hour or two on Facebook I always end up feeling as though life is a narrow set of gestures with only a few combinations at our disposal. There is one thing, though, that Facebook photos and artistic masterpieces have in common, and that is, whether you are painting a landscape or posting a picture of yourself in front of the Eiffel Tower, you are always trying to recreate something from the past, only so you can change it or force it into a new shape, or obliterate it altogether so that once the dust is settled all that is left is this depressing present that we all find to be so inadequate. When an artist paints a masterpiece (or when someone takes a picture and puts it online), they are simultaneously representing all the artists (and posters) that came before them, while they are also showing us they are completely different from these artists (and posters), and the masterpiece (or Facebook photo) they've created is something totally original. On the night of the cat incident I found myself staring at a set of photos that a friend of mine had posted after her honeymoon in Africa. They were just like all the other Facebook photos that people take while they are travelling in Africa. There were photos of my friend posing next to various animals, mostly snakes and monkeys, and making exaggerated faces of sheer terror, as if they had something to be scared of. There were nature shots – snow-capped mountains, vast prairies, even vaster deserts – where my friend would be posed next to her husband and sometimes accompanied by people who must've been guides or drivers, or they might be standing in a small group or with another couple of tourists like themselves. My friend looked extremely happy and in some of the pictures her face was literally beaming with joy. And of course there were loads of pictures of them eating, seated at a table loaded with plates and bowls piled high, a mix of glee and disbelief in their eyes, or there were photos taken after the meal, where they were posed over the dirty plates looking ridiculously pleased with themselves. When I sat there in a deep trance trolling through the photos of my friends' honeymoon in Africa, I was struck by an overpowering sense of déjà vu. Even though my friend was under the impression that she was sharing a profoundly personal experience (a life-altering trip with the love of her life), she was in fact demonstrating how deeply impersonal this experience actually was. There was nothing distinct or unique or even peculiar about her photos of her honeymoon. Basically, in these pictures, she was always mimicking other pictures (that were essentially mimicking other pictures, all the way back to . . . what?). She could have been anybody. What I ultimately find to be the core problem that all my other online problems revolve around (or more like the root problem, since all my other problems stem from it), is the way that I am constantly scanning these photos, not for very long (although I do scan over the same photos multiple times and I'm sure in some cases I've looked at the same photo what must be dozens, maybe even hundreds of times), and that I never feel any love for the people in these photographs. If I were being totally honest I'd have to admit that most of the time, as I've already said, I'm feeling envy, sadness, longing, disdain, maybe a little desire (not much though), definitely a healthy amount of full-on rage, nostalgia so strong I actually have to lie down, and in my better moments I get all wrapped up in sentimentality that kind of resembles love and affection. But I can turn this affection on and off, like the way a kid feels about their pet, a feeling that's sharp but doesn't cut very deep, so even when I stop for a second on a picture of one of my oldest friends holding her baby in her arms, a look of pure bliss on her face, and I'm able to see through my own very complex fucking feelings that a picture like this brings up, and I have a brief moment when I'm capable of thinking about something beyond my own hang-ups, all that happens is a little flash of emotion that passes through me without any lasting effect. And these moments are rare. For the most part all that looking at these pictures of my friends does is bum me out. Instead of bringing me closer to them it creates a huge distance. I see all these pictures of my friends living their lives, and even though I know it doesn't make any sense I feel like they've abandoned me. That I'm all alone. It might be someone I see all the time, like Veronica, and I may have just hung out with her a couple days before, but when I go online and look at her profile and start scanning through her pictures I feel like I no longer know her in the way I thought I did and that we're not nearly as close as I thought we were. What's worse is that my friends seem less impressive online. For instance, I think Veronica is definitely the most beautiful person I know and possibly the most beautiful person I've ever met – I'm not exaggerating – but in all of her Facebook pictures I find that her looks are only average. There's nothing special about her in any of these pictures and some of them are even unflattering. But then the next time I hang out with Veronica, after looking at her Facebook pictures, I'm immediately reminded that she is in fact as beautiful as I thought and the pictures not only didn't capture her looks but actually distorted them, just like when someone tells you that your friend, who you know to be one of the nicest people in the world, is a complete asshole, and even though when you hear gossip like this and know it's a lie, it still somehow manages to leave a mark. I remember when Jen thought Damion was cheating on her. She was convinced. But after a while she admitted she'd been feeling depressed and insecure and that Damion hadn't done anything to make her suspicious. Actually, she conceded, lately she felt he was being clingy and she was thinking they might need to take some time apart. Give each other a little space, she said. And even though I know the reason they're likely going to break up has nothing to do with Damion cheating on Jen I can't help thinking about it whenever I see them. I even hit on Damion one night after drinking half a box of wine. Since, in my mind, he'd already been unfaithful (even though he actually hadn't been), I figured, in my drunken state of mind, that he might be open to something with me.

GIVING UP

In my defense, it was a couple of months ago, when things were particularly shitty between me and James. He was spending all his time in the basement, and while I was really trying to be supportive I knew that most of the time he wasn't doing any work down there. How is it possible to spend that much time working on something without producing anything? That's what I had asked him the same night that I drank three-quarters of a box of wine and hit on Damion. The thing is, I really don't care what James does down in the basement. I really don't. As long as he's happy, I'm happy. But whenever he spends any time down there, he usually comes up looking like crap, and then he just sits on the couch with a miserable look on his face. If I try to talk to him he freaks out. Every day we go through the same routine. Whenever I suggest that we get out of the apartment, even if it's just for a walk, he gets this panicked look on his face and then goes on about how far behind he is and how he feels like he never has enough time to work. Then I tell him that I think that if he did something different to break up his usual routine it might help him relax and be more productive. I explain that the only reason I'm suggesting we go for a walk is that I'm worried about how all that time down in the basement might be affecting him. 'I know how important this is to you,' I say, 'but what's the point of spending all your time down there if you don't even like it? Even if you were able to finish what you were working on,' I say, 'I feel like you wouldn't be able to enjoy it.' Inevitably, when I talk to him like this, I end up offending him. I'm actually worried about him, and I know that most of the time he's down there all he's doing is brooding. James thinks I don't believe in him. His words. Maybe he's right, because I don't really know what he means when he accuses me of not believing in him. If he means that I don't believe it's his destiny to spend his life in our basement working away on something that nobody will ever see, then he's right. But I've never hidden that from him. It's extremely rare to succeed at what he's trying to do. I believe that he's more than capable – that maybe he's even talented – but whether he succeeds or fails doesn't really matter to me. Like I said, I just want him to be happy. So I guess in that way I do believe in him, since I believe that he's deserving of happiness. What I always say to him whenever he's freaking out and accusing me of not believing in him is that I love him. 'I love you so much,' I say. 'How is it possible for me to love you but not believe in you?' And he always answers, 'I don't know, you tell me.' On the night that I drank basically a whole box of wine I decided to fight back so I told him that he was right. 'I don't believe in you,' I said. 'I love you, but I believe that you're wasting your time down in the basement, and you're wasting my time too.' This wasn't true. I know how much his work means to him, but, to be blunt, I don't really give a shit what he does in his free time. I didn't resent him for throwing his life away on an impossible goal, I was just pissed that he had to be so miserable about it all the time. It hurt that he didn't believe me when I tried to reassure him that I didn't care whether he ever came to anything or not, and he would constantly try to provoke me and start a fight, but I knew if I admitted to what he was trying to get me to say – that he was fucking things up between us – then he'd be completely devastated. He accused me of not believing in him, but he only did this because he was fairly certain that I actually did believe in him. He's like a little boy sometimes, a little boy who thinks he's in love and constantly breaks up with his girlfriend so she'll tell him how much she loves him and wants to be with him. James needed constant reassurance, and never suspected I might get fed up one day and do the opposite, so even though he'd been baiting me for months he was pretty shocked when I told him I didn't believe in him. He stood up and went down to the basement. I caught him completely off guard. He expected me to go on about how I believed in him more than anyone else, so when I told him he'd been wasting his time (and mine) for the last seven years, that he should've done something he was 'suited for' instead of screwing around all day with no end in sight, it was as though I told him that his whole life was one big mistake. I knew what I said would hurt him, but I think I underestimated just how little he believed in himself and how much faith he'd invested in my opinion. So when I lied and told him I didn't believe in him, it was just as devastating as if I had revealed that I'd never loved him, or that I used to love him but had stopped years ago and had been faking it for almost as long as it had been for real. He was so shocked that he stood up without a word and went to the basement, and instead of chasing after him I went over to Jen and Damion's and got smashed off a box of cheap white wine and told Damion he had 'strong features' as well as many other things that I now feel really shitty about. Ever since that night we have avoided the topic of James's work in the basement, but I could tell it was bothering him, and whenever we got in an argument over how he couldn't get it up I couldn't help but feel like what we were really arguing about was how I no longer believed in his life's work. And because this had become such an issue, even though I never really thought about it before (whether I believed in James or not) ,now it was something I thought about all the time. As I sat there at my computer looking at pictures Jen and Damion had posted from the night we came close to having a threesome, I wondered if maybe James was right, and that even though I loved him I never really believed in him, which is only to say that I've never thought of what he did down in the basement as something to believe in or not to believe in. I'm being completely honest when I say that it didn't matter to me whether he was a genius or just some guy fooling around by himself in his man-cave. It's a cliché, but I love him the way he is, which doesn't mean that I don't think there isn't room for improvement in certain areas, but, just like how I've been meaning to learn an instrument, or start a small business, or take a language class, or all the other things I plan on doing but never really get around to, it didn't matter to me whether he ever got around to making any of the improvements I thought he could stand to make. That is what I meant by *fine the way he is*. Not that he's flawless, just that I've made peace with the flaws. And I don't get why he couldn't see that it didn't matter to me what he did down in the basement so long as he was happy, or why I had to constantly reassure him by saying that I believed in what

GIVING UP

he was doing. It bothered me that he didn't really understand how I felt about him, or that if he did it was cancelled out by his own doubts about himself, which were pretty severe. It was at some point during this Facebook trance that I realized the cat was in the hallway. I must've already heard something by then but I ignored it or explained it away without even being conscious of what I was explaining. Sometimes I'm able to convince myself with the most far-out explanations for something without understanding what I'm hearing or seeing or feeling. Just last month there was an earthquake. Small. Only four point five or something like that. But large enough. I had just put some water on to boil when everything started to shake. If you've been through one then you know what it's like. The closest comparison I can think of would be having a train pass right by your bedroom window, but without the train noise, and since I wasn't *expecting* an earthquake – they never happen here or anywhere else I've lived, and this was my first – I thought that what was happening was anything *except* an earthquake. The first thing that occurred to me was that the water must be boiling so much that it was shaking the kitchen. This, of course, is insane. But this is the sort of stuff I come up with. I had put the water on not even a minute before so it was impossible that it had already started to boil, and even it if were possible there's no way that a boiling kettle can shake a kitchen, let alone an entire building – which was what was really happening – the way that an earthquake can. I immediately realized how crazy it was to think that the kettle was the reason for what was happening, but my next idea was just as ridiculous – I thought that my neighbours were doing laundry. I even listened for the sound of a dryer coming through the walls, but I eventually realized that this was just as stupid as the kettle theory. By that point I was panicking because I couldn't make sense of what was going on and just as I was considering whether it was a low-flying plane, the shaking stopped, and just as abruptly I stopped thinking about what had happened. I should've been at least mildly disturbed. I should've checked online at least, but I didn't think about it again until the next morning when I was listening to the radio and I found out that it *had* been an earthquake. I was shocked. An earthquake – and I had tried to explain it away by a boiling kettle, or a loud dryer, or a low-flying plane, and when each of these didn't hold up, I simply forgot about it. It reminded me of this time I had seen a couple arguing outside of a club and then read in the paper, the next day that a woman had been murdered outside of a club by her boyfriend. I was sure that the woman I had seen was the murder victim in the paper and for a moment I considered calling the police, but I eventually let it go. I feel like this happens all the time, all this tragic shit is going on and most of the time we don't even know it. The moment you walk out the door there's a very good chance you're going to pass someone on the street who is going through a serious crisis. But most of the time you walk by without even noticing. It's like that story Veronica told me about somebody she works with who was living next to a dead guy for a month. Apparently she'd just moved in and met her neighbour in the hallway that night and then never saw him again. She never heard him either, even though the previous tenant had warned her that the walls were thin. Every night she watched TV in her apartment she would wonder why she couldn't hear anything coming from the other side of the wall. Then she noticed a smell. At first she thought it might be a plumbing issue, but when she called and complained they sent someone to check and nothing was wrong with her pipes. The smell didn't go away though and eventually she called again to complain and this time the super decided to check next door. She was with him when he let himself into the apartment and they found her neighbour's body decomposing in his bed. But it doesn't even have to be that dramatic. You might find out that someone you worked with was going through the worst time of their life, and when you look back through your memory to see if you missed something, it doesn't take long to realize how obvious it should've been that they were in pain. It's not that you're ignorant about what goes on in other people's lives, it's just that you've got your own shit to worry about. When the cat first came through the front window screen I ignored it. More specifically, I thought to myself, 'That must be coming from next door.' But then I heard something else, a breathing or sneezing sound. I knew right away that it belonged to a cat. Our street was crawling with them. Since we'd moved in there'd been a couple of cat incidents. James liked to keep the screen open in the basement because he said he needed fresh air, but this meant that our neighbour's cat would stroll in. After the second time he came into our kitchen we started keeping the screens shut. Now, I thought, the sounds had initially come from the front room. It was definitely a sneezing sound that I was hearing. I found myself wondering what sort of diseases cats can pass on to humans. I was pretty sure rabies was one of them. I felt sick to my stomach all of a sudden. The idea of a rabid animal in my apartment was literally sickening. I have nothing against cats. We had one growing up. I've never thought about getting one but I understand the appeal – they're cute. To each their own, I guess, but since our neighbour's cat started coming into our place I've been having nightmares of my bed being invaded. Needless to say, the moment I heard the sound of a sneezing cat in the front room I prayed it would go away. And for a moment, when the sneezing stopped, I even managed to convince myself that it had gone back out the window. Then the sneezing started up again and I knew that I was going to have to do something. There was a part of me that was considering all sorts of fucked-up possibilities, scenarios that were horrifying and totally realistic. But I never gave them any serious consideration, and they didn't develop beyond a flurry of sensations that crowded out my thoughts, like the way that darkness surrounds the headlights of an approaching car, so you only focus on what you can see, and take it on faith that nothing is going to come hurtling out of the darkness and throw itself in your way. Since my neighbour's cat had come into my apartment before, it was understandable to suspect that the noises I heard were coming from him, or from a stray in the alley out back, so I naturally ignored my more irrational fears (like a home intruder) and zeroed in on the cat theory. I grabbed the broom from the kitchen and ran back just in time to catch the cat coming into the hallway. All the lights were out except for the reading lamp by the couch where'd I'd been sitting, and the glow from the laptop that I'd put on the coffee table, still open on Veronica's Facebook page. I didn't recognize the cat. It was puffy and dark and moving slowly, but not with the usual alert caution, that way they have when they are exploring a new place – this was more like the weary movements of a cow, a sort of slow plodding that freaked me out. I expected the cat to be afraid of me but it kept coming at me. It kept its head low and swung it side to side, which only enhanced its resemblance to a cow, and I could see that there was something hanging from its mouth. At this point, I realized that it was making a sucking sound, like a drooling baby with a mouthful of candy. The thing in its mouth was limp and dark and stringy. All at once I felt a revolting mix of anger and pity. I assumed it had caught a mouse and that the sucking sound was something it did when it was excited, or that this was the sound cats made when they held mice in their jaws, and the reason it was coming right at me without any sign of fear was that it was proud of itself and was showing off its catch. Some of my friends own cats and I've heard them tell stories about waking up to find a bird on their pillow, or finding a mouse resting on the welcome mat as they are on their way out the door to work, but this wasn't my cat, and it didn't look anything like the neighbour's cat, which was smaller and had shorter hair, so why would it bring a mouse into my apartment? I wanted it to go away. Why did it pick my apartment? Why didn't it bring this mouse to somebody else? Even now that it was in my apartment, why couldn't it tell that I was angry and scared? Why didn't it leave? I thought cats and dogs were supposed to be all in tune with people's emotions. Not this one. It just kept coming at me with that stupid walk, making that gross Silence of the Lambs sucking noise. I started yelling at it to keep back but it actually started coming even faster. I stuck the broom out and pushed it into its face. Instead of scurrying away like I expected, she collapsed face-first onto the floor. Her movements were so clumsy, not like any cat I had ever seen. I was literally horrified. Like pretty much everybody else in the world, I have a deep fear of anything unusual. I know it's not cool to admit to that sort of thing. Everyone likes to pretend that they don't get freaked out by stuff that is out of the ordinary, but of course most people do get freaked out when they see something weird, or gross. At least I can admit it. Whenever I see someone with a deformity I can't help but be completely terrified. I know it's wrong, and that someone with a deformity is just as natural, or as freakish, as someone who's perfectly normal, but knowing this doesn't seem to change how I feel about it. There was something *off* about the way the cat reacted when I shoved the broom in its face. I wouldn't have been able to articulate it then, but now I would say that it seemed indifferent, or at least it seemed unafraid, which freaked me out. I tried to sweep it towards the kitchen – my plan was to kick it out the back door – but it flattened itself to the floor and as I was trying to push it forward it managed to squeeze itself under the couch. This only made me crazier. 'This *thing* thinks it can just stroll into my apartment with a bloody mouse in its jaws and hide out under my couch,' I thought. 'Like I don't have enough problems already, now I have to deal with some feral animal that's all high from killing a mouse?' I got down and jammed the broom under the couch. I could feel the weight of the thing against the handle, but I didn't look to see where it was. I didn't want to see it. The way it hung its head and the look of the bloody mess in its jaws made me nauseous. Even as I was crouched down on the floor trying to pry it from under the couch I was already remembering the image of the cat – whose head, I now realized, had a weird, box-like shape to it – and while the actual moment only lasted a second, it felt like I now had the ability to pause the image and examine it with the sort of deep focus of a witness who, after a crime has been committed, is brought in to stare at a series of photos, or a composite sketch, or maybe even the actual face of the suspect, so that they can take all the time in the world to figure out what it was (and who it was) that they really saw. Back in the hallway, when the cat was coming towards me, I'd been so freaked out I almost ran out the back door. Somehow I managed to overcome this urge, but, once I did, the next thought I had was to get the cat out of the apartment. I experienced all of this before I even really saw the cat. Everything happened all at once, and at some point I focussed in on the thing dangling from its mouth. I remember thinking to myself, 'What *is* that?' and then I immediately decided, 'It must be a mouse.' But as I was trying to pry her loose (she'd turned on her back and dug her claws into the bottom of the couch), I found myself stuck on this image of the cat coming towards me in the hallway. At the same time as I was frantically trying to get the cat out the back door, I was calmly reviewing the memory of my initial encounter with the cat just seconds before, and, just as I felt it give way a bit, I realized that the thing in the cat's mouth didn't look anything like a mouse. For a second I almost stopped. I probably let up a bit. The cat was desperate to stay under the couch. I could feel her fighting against the broom. The truth is, I wasn't doing a good job – I didn't have a very good grip on the broom so I couldn't put a lot of strength into it – and even though I desperately wanted the cat out of the apartment, a very significant part of me was scared to have to see it again. I managed to drag her to the edge of the couch. This was strange too. On the one hand, it was obviously desperate to stay hidden and was doing everything it could to resist the broom, but on the other hand it seemed listless, like its heart wasn't in the fight, and I remember thinking that for a stray cat it wasn't very wild. Where was the snarling? The hissing? I'd seen cats in fights – they go crazy. They flail and squirm and basically turn into little tornadoes of panic and fury. This one was almost limp, as if she'd more or less given up and was only making a show of resisting when it was actually looking forward to being captured, or killed (since I expect that most animals, no matter how domesticated, always assume that when someone comes at them with a broom it's because they plan on killing them). I couldn't understand why it was so intent to stay under my couch when to do so meant fending off my broom attack, and even though I was terrified of the cat's oddly shaped head and the bloody mass in its mouth, and had to fight the urge just to run out of the apartment and wait for James to get back and take care of it, I could feel a sense of outrage building up inside of me. It doesn't make any sense, really, but I felt that the way this cat had invaded my apartment was totally unfair. I realize that 'fairness' doesn't really apply to the behaviour of stray cats and that it was just as ridiculous to take offense if it rains when you're on vacation. You spend your days in the hotel room trying not to let it get to you but it's impossible not to feel like life is messing with you, testing you, or even that the actual weather was conspiring against you, as if nature was something with a personality, and was being a bit of a prick. I know how narcissistic this must sound, and I know that the cat didn't come into my apartment because of some grand design, or in order to torment me, or as a sign or symbol of my fate, but that it picked my place at random (well, almost at random, since James must've opened the window before he went on his break). There's a huge gap between knowing something is true and actually believing it, and at that moment what I truly believed in my heart of hearts was that this cat was deliberately messing with me, or that someone had sent it in order to mess with me. Of course nobody was messing with me, it was just bad luck, for the both of us, especially for the cat, who thought she might be safe in my apartment (the chances were in her favour since this is a cat-friendly neighbourhood and I expect most people wouldn't have re- acted the way I did), but now that I was crushing it with a broom she was obviously afraid for her life. She was terrified that once she was out in the open I would catch her and kill her. This was all that was going on. Just a frightened stray. But I didn't believe it – or maybe I kind of believed it, but I definitely didn't *feel* it. What I felt was that after a shitty day, which was part of a series of shitty days making up a parade of shitty months (maybe even *years*), when I could've really used some sort of sign that things were going to get better and that life wasn't going to turn out to be a random series of disappointments, was the precise moment that capital-L Life decided to send me a sign. A scary one. I started going at the cat pretty hard. Up until that point I'd been trying to *reason* with her – mind you I was reasoning with a broom, but still I was trying more to coax her out rather than to force her. All of that changed. I could feel myself giving in, or letting go. I was giving in to the disgust I felt for the cat. A powerful revulsion had been rising within me the moment I set eyes on the thing but I'd been fighting to keep it down. I knew that if I gave in to this feeling I would go berserk and trash my apartment, or something even worse. Once I let go of my fear over what I might do to my apartment, or myself, or the cat, then it was easy, a relief even, to give in to the overpowering disgust that was coursing through my veins. If you've ever seen a child who's been bullied finally snap and turn on her tormenters then you'll have a pretty good idea of what I looked like – screaming over and over again, something along the lines of 'Get out! Get the fuck out! Get out!' while I chopped and sliced with the broom in a total frenzy. I'm only exaggerating slightly

GIVING UP

when I say that, for a moment, I lost my mind. But it worked. The cat crawled out from under the couch. She was making that sucking noise again, except now it was louder and she was wheezing as well, or at least I think that's what it was, since it was faint and disembodied, as if the wheezing was coming from another cat hiding in my bedroom (and even though I knew that this was ridiculous I definitely considered it for a second, which should give you some idea of how messed up my thinking was by that point). I was standing between her and the kitchen. I smacked the broom down in front of her a few times and when she froze I swung as hard as I could. She literally flew through the air. This took me a bit by surprise, even though what happened was more or less what I'd intended (except it's not accurate to say that I *intended* anything at all – I just swept the cat towards the kitchen with everything I had, and I don't remember thinking of what the result would be). I watched with a sort of creeping awareness as the cat sailed through the air and slammed into the kitchen table. It had splayed out while it was flying through the air, so it hit the table and then crumpled to the floor. I thought of a Frisbee, when it wobbles through the air before bouncing off a tree and spinning into the ground. The cat smacked into the table leg and I remember thinking to myself, 'You killed her.' I'd been lying to myself about why the cat was acting so weird, and what it was that was hanging from its mouth. I'd been so freaked out and scared that it wasn't until I watched the cat spasm in pain when it struck the table leg that I became aware of what I'd actually known since it crawled under the couch.

And it wasn't until I said to myself, 'You killed her,' that I knew that I knew. The cat was obviously severely injured, most likely because it'd been hit by a car. I stood there with the broom in my hands. She scrambled to her feet and then ran out the kitchen door as fast as her little broken body could move. I ran to the door but she was already down the stairs, though I seriously doubt that I would've gone after her, since, now that I knew the shiny mass dangling from her mouth wasn't a little dead mouse but most likely the cat's brains or guts, and that the reason she had such a weird shape to her head was that her skull had been crushed, I was even more horrified, and just the thought of what I might see if I got close enough to pick the thing up actually made me nauseous. As I was standing there at the kitchen door the whole incident started flashing through my mind. Now that I knew the cat was seriously injured it seemed almost insane that I could've mistaken the stuff pouring out of its mouth for a dead mouse. I flicked the kitchen light on and at the spot by the table where she had landed there was a splatter of blood that trailed to the kitchen door, and when I went back to the TV room and turned on the lights I saw a trail of blood from the hallway that led to the couch where it turned into a smear (which must have been where I hit her with the broom). I followed the blood down the hall and, while I'd been right – James *had* left the window open – I saw that the screen had been shut, and the cat had torn through it. She had been hit by a car and then ran to the first open window she could find, and even when the screen was closed, she had torn though it. She had been looking for somewhere safe where she could hide and instead she was beat up by a crazy woman with a broom. The poor little thing was terrified and no doubt in a lot of pain and I had turned it back out into the street. 'And the worst thing is,' I thought, 'I knew what I was doing the entire time.'

JAMES AND MARY

The only light in the apartment is the bluish illumination coming from the computer screen at the end of the hall. He doesn't turn the lights on because he doesn't want Mary to know that he's home, at least not until he has had time to *compose himself*, but after taking off his shoes he ends up tripping over the broom. The broom is totally unexpected and completely invisible to him, something about its place in the hallway is incongruous and even disturbing. Still, his reaction as it clatters to the floor is a bit over the top, as if he's been surprised by something much more perilous. 'Motherfuck!' he says. 'Jesus motherfucking Christ on the fucking cross. I'm going to have a fucking aneurysm. What is this?' he picks up the broom. 'A fucking broom?' Mary, sitting at the computer, waits for his little fit to pass. As it happens, by not saying anything to him she actually hastens the process. He eventually calms down, takes a seat on the couch, places the broom across his lap, and asks in his best imitation of a casual tone whether she was doing some light cleaning while he was out. But she doesn't respond and he wonders if maybe she's looking at something disturbing or reading an email with some bad news about a close friend or family member, her parents even. A look at the screen confirms that she's just doing what she usually does when she's bored or tired, which is look at her friends' profiles on Facebook. She asks him if he had a nice break and he says that he did and that he's feeling refreshed and ready to get back to work. Sometimes that's all he needs, just to get away for a bit and clear his head, because when he's down there for too long it's like he gets too close to what he's working on and he can't see it anymore, like his face is pressed up to the TV screen, or to the pages of a book, so just by getting out and seeing other people he is able to get a little distance and put 'the work' back in the right perspective. She wants to know if other people were out walking around at midnight on a Tuesday. She wonders why it takes two hours to get some distance and regain his perspective. When he had said 'seeing other people,' he explains, it didn't mean that he'd been walking around and staring at strangers, it was a figure of speech, and he doesn't normally go for two-hour walks, but it's a nice night and he was feeling cramped down there in the basement so he ended up staying out longer than usual. 'Well,' she says, 'a cat came into the apartment while you were gone.' He asks her what she means when she says that a cat came into the apartment. The look that she gives him before he's even done asking this question shows that while this is exactly what she's been expecting him to ask, she is still disappointed to hear him say it, since she thinks that this sort of thing is beneath him. Why, she wonders, does he pretend that he doesn't understand what she meant when she said that a cat came into the apartment, when he actually knows exactly what she is talking about? Why does he act like he's not intensely aware of everything that's going on around him when she knows for a fact that he is extremely sensitive and notices the most insignificant details and is basically the most perceptive person she's ever met? What is the point of making her explain herself when he already knows what she is going to say? But he insists that he honestly doesn't know what she's talking about, and even if he is as perceptive as she says, which he doesn't think is the case, then all this means is that he'd noticed she is obviously upset about something (a complete stranger would've picked up on it), and that when she said that a cat came into the apartment he could tell she was holding something back, something much worse than a cat coming into the apartment. There's literally no way he could know what she had meant because no matter how observant he might be or how well they know each other after all these years, he isn't Sherlock fucking Holmes, not even close, so at the end of the day the only way he could know was if she told him, which she hadn't, not yet. She gives him the same look as before and says that he's still pretending to misunderstand her, which at this point is just kind of mean. She knows that it is impossible for him to know *exactly* what happened. But he knew that *something* had happened, so why did she feel like if she hadn't said anything that he would've never asked her what was wrong? Why does he make her feel like he is doing her a favour by listening to her? And why does he ask her what she means when she tells him that a cat came into the apartment, when he should really be asking her if she was all right? Had Mary chased it out, or had she run into their bedroom and waited for it to leave on its own? This is, of course, what he'd meant by his question, he explains. It's a figure of speech. 'Everything that comes out of your mouth is a figure of speech,' she says. It seems to him more than a little ironic that at the same time as she's accusing him of playing dumb this is more or less exactly what she's doing. 'Anyway,' he says, 'I'm sorry about the way I phrased my question. What I meant to say was how did the cat get in, and were you able to chase it out, and, if not, where is it now?' 'Well,' she says, 'he came in through the front window.' 'How?' he wonders. 'Wasn't the screen closed?' 'It was, but she pushed through it.' Now it is his turn to get frustrated. Something had obviously happened while he'd been on his break and he doesn't understand why she won't just tell him. In response to this little outburst she stands up and turns on the lights so he can see the blood that is smeared all over the floor. 'Jesus fucking Christ,' he says. 'What the hell happened in here?' She starts to explain what had happened and he tries to listen to her patiently but she is very upset, the sight of the blood is disturbing and she keeps checking behind her as if she's worried the cat is going to come back somehow, and instead of just starting her story at the moment the cat came through the window, she begins at the moment he left for his break, so he has to listen as she describes how she wasted two hours fucking around on Facebook. She has a hard time getting her story out because she keeps on interrupting herself in order to insert completely extraneous details that mean absolutely nothing to him, but that are clearly very significant to her. It never occurs to her that what she is saying is irrelevant and even distracting because for her these details are crucial to understanding what happened. If she had just said, 'A cat broke through the screen in the front window and, before I realized that what I thought was a mouse hanging out of her mouth was probably blood and maybe even its brains, I had already chased her out the kitchen door with the broom,' then he wouldn't have been able to appreciate her experience of the cat incident. He understands that the experience isn't confined to the time the cat was actually in the apartment, that it extends to what was going on before, and what came afterwards, but all he wants to hear about right now is the cat. 'I can tell you're upset, and I know it must've been crazy to turn around and see something like that in the apartment,' he says, after he's interrupted her in the midst of describing her best friend's Facebook photos, 'and I don't want you to think that I'm cutting you off. I want to hear everything. But it's just that you are so clearly shaken up, and there's blood all over the place. I need to know what happened. Can we please just skip to the part about the cat, and then you can go back and fill everything else in?' She's irritated and embarrassed by his interruption. He said that she was upset, but what he means is that she is *losing control*. She's rambling. She's hysterical. She can't see that what is important right now is to tell him about the cat incident so he can make a calm, rational decision about what they should do next. Her experience of the cat incident – how she felt and what she was thinking at the time – is not important. At least not now. Not yet. It is of secondary importance. But since she is so upset she is confusing these secondary issues with the primary ones, which were, in order of importance – did something happen to her? to the apartment? and, finally, to the cat? Once the primary issues were out of the way, he meant to say, they could focus on the lesser issues (i.e. her experience of the cat incident). And she's embarrassed because she suspects that he's right, that she should just get to the point, and that including all the extraneous detail about wasting her night on Facebook is betraying all sorts of things that really have nothing to do with the cat incident. So she pauses for a second, and then starts again at the moment that she saw the cat in the hallway. But now she's having a hard time getting through her story because James keeps interrupting her with questions that seem to her to be completely beside the point. He wants to know the colour of the cat and its size, whether it hissed at her or if the hair on its back was sticking up. This is extremely irritating, and with each interruption she tells him that if he will just let her finish then he can ask her anything afterwards, but he explains that he can't help himself. He starts asking the question before he can remember that she had already asked him to 'save his questions to the end.' 'Besides,' he continues, 'they just occur to me, and if I didn't ask then I'd probably forget what they were.' She suggests that if he forgets what they were then they probably weren't worth asking in the first place. He replies that he didn't think it works that way. 'Just because a question isn't asked, doesn't mean it shouldn't be answered,' he says. And because she finds this sort of sententious horseshit even more irritating than having to answer his irritating questions, she tries to keep her temper in check and refrain from arguing the point any further, and instead just answers with as few words as possible. She had heard the cat before she saw it but she didn't know what it was at first. She noticed the thing hanging from its mouth right away. She had thought it was a mouse, but knew that it wasn't, if that makes any sense. It hit the kitchen table with its side, not its head. 'It must've only been grazed if it still had the strength to tear through the screen,' he says. She isn't stupid. She knows what he is implying – that maybe the cat wasn't seriously injured when it came into the apartment and that she'd only messed it up more with the broom. 'I can't believe you're doing this,' she says. 'The *whole point* to my story was that I should've noticed that the cat was all messed up the moment I saw it, but since I was still in a fucking Facebook trance I didn't realize what I was seeing.' She went on to say that he habitually misses the point of everything she tries to tell him, and on top of that he typically doubts her version of events. He always suspects that she is keeping something from him, or even more often that she simply doesn't know what the fuck is going on. 'You must have a pretty low opinion of me,' she says, 'if you think that I'm that stupid or delusional.' He says that she's exaggerating when she says that he *always* doubts what she tells him, and it isn't true that he thinks she is stupid or delusional, but under the circumstances it would've been perfectly understandable if she didn't remember things exactly the way they happened. 'With all the lights off it's pretty dark in here,' he says, 'especially if you've been staring at a computer screen. Your vision is going to be pretty fucked,' he lowers his voice, 'and you may not realize it but I don't think I've ever seen you this worked up before.' He realizes that he is standing up while she is still sitting at the computer desk, so he's literally talking down to her. He takes a seat on the couch. 'I'm not saying you're delusional, but you even said that you were freaked out and weren't really thinking straight. I'm just trying to think things through and consider all the possibilities.' He pauses, and then they both stand and walk slowly to the kitchen door. She stays inside while he goes onto the patio and checks out the alley. 'Nothing,' he says, and comes back inside. 'Listen,' she says, 'you're not making sense. There's

GIVING UP

no way a healthy cat tore through our screen and injured itself in the process. And that doesn't matter anyway because I *did* see it, I just didn't know what I was looking at until it was too late.' She sits at the kitchen table and starts reciting the events of the cat incident as though she is working out a difficult problem in front of an audience – an audience that she's not really aware of anymore because she's so involved in what she's trying to figure out, but then she loses her focus and can feel herself being watched and falters and gives up. 'This is ridiculous,' she says, 'I don't even know why I'm even considering this for a second. I know what I saw. I know what happened. I was there. And I don't know why this is so important to you anyway. Why does it matter that it got hit by a car or tore itself open on our screen? Which, by the way, doesn't even seem possible – to cut itself up on a screen so badly that it pours blood all over the floor? But who cares? What does it matter what caused it to bleed all over the place?' She keeps looking out the window, and so does James, who is leaning against the door and basically staring outside while Mary asks him these questions in a genuinely bewildered tone of voice. 'Well,' he says, 'I guess if he just cut himself on our screen then he probably isn't seriously injured. But if he got hit by a car, that would probably mean that he's really fucked up.' She seems to consider one last time whether there might be something to what he is saying and then answers, 'No, there was definitely something wrong with it. Its head was a weird shape and its fucking brain was coming out of its mouth.' He turns off the outdoor light but continues to stare out the window. 'It *is* possible he's down in the alley,' he says. 'I should maybe go check.' This is unquestionably the right thing to do, but she almost tells him not to go. It probably *is* out there, curled up under the patio, trying to breathe, maybe drowning in its own blood, but if James finds it what is he going to do? Bring it inside? Take it to a vet? Save its life? 'What's the point?' she thinks, but immediately regrets it and feels ashamed because she knows that finding the cat is the right thing to do. 'James always does the right thing,' she says to herself. 'That's his thing. More than anything else, he's obsessed with doing the right thing,' she thinks. Or maybe it isn't that he always does the right thing, but that he never willingly does the wrong thing. If he suspects there is even a slight chance of doing the wrong thing then he can't go through with it. So since it's a compulsive form of behaviour, and he's helpless to do anything other than the right thing, it's pretty hard to give him full credit for it. If anything, it's a deficiency. Like the time they found a wallet on the beach and it felt like it would've been fun to take the cash since they were still young and broke, but not only would he have nothing to do with her suggestion, he wouldn't simply leave it where it was so that its owner, once he realized he'd lost it, could return to retrieve it, or, what was more likely, so that someone else less obsessed with doing the right thing could find it and steal it. Instead he literally combed the beach in search of the owner. They could never just drive by a car if it looked like it was stranded on the highway. He always pulled over to *see if they could help*, even if it meant postponing or even cancelling their own plans. At first she thought he was doing this out of a perverse sense of pride, a sort of minor martyrdom, and that eventually he'd find some other way to satisfy this misplaced belief in his superiority, maybe even by doing the exact opposite and only ever acting in his own self-interest. Then she thought maybe he was acting out of a sense of inferiority, and by never doing the wrong thing he was fulfilling his need to deny himself, and to punish himself for every time he put himself before someone else, especially if that someone was a complete stranger. If either of these scenarios were true, however, then in the same way that his sense of superiority and inferiority fluctuated wildly from day to day (and even within each day), this obsession with doing the right thing should be more unbalanced. And if *this* were true, when the opportunity came where he had a clear choice between right and wrong, he might not feel the need to prove himself one way or another, and whether he did the right thing or not would be left to more pressing concerns, so that he might end up doing the *wrong thing* for the sake of convenience. But this *never* happened, which led her to suspect that there's no coherent psychological explanation for his behaviour and that it is likely just a habit, or ingrained familial superstition, like the way two sisters insist on sleeping against the wall because this was the position they fought for when they were young and were forced to share a bed, and even though they are now all grown up and the people they share their beds with are indifferent to what side they sleep on, they still get nervous when asking respective partners if they mind sleeping on the far side of the bed. James, unsurprisingly, was oblivious to this unfailing compulsion to do the right thing, since, unlike Mary, he didn't view his behaviour from the same God-like perspective from which all the discrete actions he took throughout his life could be seen at a glance, the way that a city can be taken in from an airplane so that all the individual features cohere and all that you can see is the vast structure or system always at work governing the life of the city, yet remaining hidden or invisible to the people on the ground. Instead, to James, every choice is unique, and he would've been offended if Mary told him that she knew what he was going to decide before he did. He felt like he struggled with his decision every time he made one. The cat is probably a block away right now, or, if it is under the patio, is James really going to crawl under there and get it? And it may not even be injured, or at least not as bad as Mary thought it was. But if it is as bad as she thinks it is, then he is going to have to bring an extremely traumatized and broken animal to a clinic (if there is even one open at this time of night) just so they can kill it 'humanely,' which no doubt is going to cost him a couple hundred dollars. Not only would his night of working be completely shot, but all the excitement and subsequent exhaustion would prevent him from working tomorrow as well. 'I'll just go outside and take a quick look,' he says, 'just to make sure he's not laying out there suffering or anything like that.' He couldn't help adding that little dig at the end because even though it makes absolutely no sense, he blames Mary for this infuriating distraction from his life's work. 'First the con man, now the cat,' he says to himself, as if these two incidents perfectly express the condition of their lives at that moment, even though they are in fact unrelated, but putting them into a single phrase, and uttering it silently, illuminates a shared quality, an offbeat affinity that has nothing to do with reason, like the rhymes in a nonsense poem that seem ridiculous on the page but make a strange sort of sense when you read them out loud. He goes out onto the patio and stands at the railing and pretends to search for the cat. Even though Mary hadn't done anything to bring the cat incident about, and even if it was a total fluke that the cat had chosen their apartment over someone else's, he couldn't shake the feeling that she is somehow responsible. It isn't something he'd ever utter out loud, or even allow to the surface of his thoughts, but somewhere below in the grim basement of his mind he keeps hidden the suspicion that her carelessness is to blame for a lot of the things that go wrong in their lives. The irony being that it is precisely this quality that had attracted him to her in the first place. Instead of endlessly scrutinizing every detail, each possible outcome, the countless interpretations of each aspect of daily life, she threw herself into things and simply trusted that they would fall into place. 'What's the worst thing that could happen?' she would say. If she was picking something up at the store, she left the car running outside, and she might strike up a conversation with the cashier and end up leaving it running for half an hour. One day, on his way home from work, James saw her car idling outside their local coffee shop and, in order to *teach her a lesson*, he hopped in and drove home. But when she got home a few minutes later she didn't even make a remark. 'Weren't you afraid someone stole the car,' he asked. 'No,' she said, 'I just assumed you took it as a lame joke in order to teach me a lesson or something like that.' 'But somebody could have stolen it,' he insisted. 'Yes,' she said, 'but they didn't.' He couldn't help but admire how utterly unconcerned she was with the fundamentals, the sort of *life skills* that everyone needs to be able to make it through the day. Because not only did she make it through the day – she thrived. Let's say they're going out to eat but they get to the restaurant just as it's closing – James would suggest they go somewhere else, whereas Mary would plead with the hostess, who'd initially be hostile but eventually warm to her, so that by the end of the night they would be sitting at the bar with the rest of the staff, eating and drinking for free. It's obvious why James would find this attractive, but there's a less romantic side to this sort of character. She is never surprised when everything works out, but if something goes wrong, she is outraged. He'd noticed this early on but it wasn't until she bought a couch on a whim and then fell to pieces when it turned out to be too big to fit through their doorway that he started to keep score. She developed a bitter impatience with their apartment after that, and within a few more months she told him she couldn't 'live in this shithole any longer' and they had to move. And then, after she tried to flush a bag of potting soil down the toilet, they had to move from that apartment too. So even though she insists that the cat came through the front window he can't help but suspect that there's something more to her story. 'She doesn't *mean* to distract me from my life's work,' he thinks, 'but whether she means to or not, and whether she's responsible or not, this sort of thing happens all the time.' He is constantly being distracted by trivial incidents that end up getting completely out of hand and swallowing up all the time and energy he puts aside every day in order to bring the seemingly endless project a little closer to completion. He looks over the railing and stares into the darkness. Mary is supposed to be the practical one, level-headed, so he is freshly disappointed whenever something like the cat incident happens, because he realizes that she is just as ill-prepared for the demands that reality is constantly making as he is. He stares into the alley and listens for the sounds of an injured cat, whatever that is supposed to sound like, but it's quiet. Usually their neighbours stay up late drinking and playing loud music, or have people over for large dinner parties, talking and laughing until one of the other neighbours yells at them to keep it down. And when they first moved in, he had been so sure of himself and his life's work (that he'd only just started) that instead of interfering with his progress, all this street noise and the sounds of the other people living in the building served as a form of accompaniment. But all that is over now, and even the slightest noise from outside is enough to cause irritation, which then quickly grows into full-blown anger, and finally, obsession. He is no longer sure of himself and what he is doing. It's all so precarious and uncertain. He is terrified of failing, of never finishing his life's work, and when he is sequestered in the basement, trying to get something done, and the bullying sound of an action movie or the mewling of a distressed cat comes pouring in through the basement window and works its way into his thoughts, so that he ends up sitting and staring in a distracted stupor, he worries that he doesn't have the talent for concentration that he needs if he is ever going to accomplish anything. In the same way that he is distracted by the very background noise that used to accompany him, he is also irritated by the household sounds that used to cheer him up and sustain him throughout the drudgery of his life's work. Not that long ago, he liked to think about what Mary was up to while he was down in the basement. 'Here I am,' he would think, 'working away at my life's work while she goes about the work of living.' The sounds she made as she moved around upstairs complimented the virtual silence of his sedentary work in the basement. It was a sort of symbiosis, the way they both kept to their respective spaces in the apartment and simultaneously worked away at their respective tasks, with the shared goal of living a fulfilled and contented life. Of course, neither of them had ever gone so far as to say this goal out loud, but it was understood, and he felt like they had the same unspoken agreement with respect to his life's work. They were both committed to its completion, and even though she never directly involved herself in it, there was never a question that everything she did upstairs was in service of the work he was doing below. He would imagine what a biographer might write about them if he ever finished his work and his genius was finally recognized. They would point out that he would've never been able to accomplish something so monumental without the tireless and practical assistance of his wife, Mary. Without her, they would say, it's unlikely that James would've ever started out on such an ambitious endeavour, let alone have finished it. James would sit for hours in the basement absorbed in his demanding work but he could always be sure that once he tore himself away he would emerge into domestic calm. Her work was as particular and short-term as his was abstract and unending. Together they sustained and inspired one another, because, just as Mary's activities upstairs served as an ongoing endorsement for the complete shambles he referred to as his life's work, so James's time in the basement elevated the sense of significance and purpose in the work that kept Mary busy throughout the day. Listening to Mary getting supper ready in the kitchen spurned him on to get a little more work done before it was time to eat. When she started watching TV after dinner he knew that he only had a couple of hours before she would call down to him to come join her for the tea that they drank together every night before she went to bed, leaving him with another two hours to *unwind* by half-reading a book or screwing around online. He set his routines by hers. Whenever she was gone for the night and he had the place to himself he found it impossible to get any work done. Because he had started his life's work before he met Mary he never considered that one day she might become integral to it. In the beginning, when they moved in together and he'd been obliged to establish a new set of work habits in order to accommodate his radically new living situation, he worried that he'd been naive about what was involved with sharing a space – maybe living together would become a distraction, or even a full-on obstruction to getting any work done. Now that they had established the routines which have been in place for years, he no longer saw her as impeding his work, although he didn't exactly credit her with assisting him either, instead he congratulated himself for being able to work in spite of her presence. Of course, since he's more or less convinced that he is a failure, he's fallen into thinking she is somehow preventing him from getting anything done. Before, when the floor creaked under her feet, or the muffled waterworks ran overhead as she washed the dishes, he'd reflect on how well they shared their living space, or how perfectly their arrangement was working. But now the sounds of her banging around in the kitchen puts him in a rage. It is as if she waits for the precise moment that he finally buckles down and starts getting some work done, after he's wasted the first few hours in the basement avoiding this very thing – work – while she spends the lead-up to this moment in perfect silence, reading a book on the couch or flipping through a magazine or messing around online, and then, once he's finally got himself into a state where he's capable of taking another crack at his life's work, she gets up from whatever it is she's been doing, and starts making a racket right over his head. He used to think, 'This is how it should be. While I'm working towards the completion of my *life's work*, she sustains our life together, she fills up all the empty hours I spend down in the basement with the business of *ordinary life*. We have worked out the *ideal conditions*,' he used to think, 'for accomplishing something of lasting importance.' Once he started to worry, however, that he may never actually achieve his goal, he began to notice the ways that their domestic arrangement fell short of fulfilling this supposedly symbiotic system. He suspected that there was, in fact, no unspoken agreement or domestic truce, and that their home life was made up of a random clutch of mindless activities and last-minute solutions that barely maintained the illusion of order. Mary is just as focussed on impractical, abstract, and unlikely goals as he is. Just as James spends his time in the basement consumed by a project that has no basis in reality, so Mary spends hours upstairs planning *their* future – a future that has just as much to do with the present as James's hoped-for success has to do with what he's accomplished so far. It's also not entirely true that Mary concerns herself with the day-to-day necessities while James works on his grandly unnecessary and abstract life's work, because he actually pitches in quite a bit. It is James who cleans the house, deals with the landlord, handles the bills, runs most of the errands, and all the other things that Mary is unwilling to do or feels are more appropriate for him. Her role and duties aren't as clearly defined, but while it's never been stated outright, and even though James takes care of the lion's share, it is clearly through Mary's guidance and supervision that the *order* of their lives is maintained, and until now James had always

been happy with this arrangement, but he's starting to resent it, so when he is down in the basement trying to get
some work done and Mary starts banging around in the
kitchen, no doubt making banana bread or something
equally superfluous, instead of cleaning out the fridge (like
she's been promising to do for weeks) or getting dinner
ready (her only regular task – and one she often put off or
neglects until they're both so hungry that James ends up
going to pick up some takeout at the Indian place down the
street), he tells himself that she's the reason that he'll never
finish his life's work. It's not lost on Mary that he blames
her for distracting him. She can tell by the way he's standing out there on the balcony that he's furious over the cat
incident. He's pretending to look for it but all he's really
doing is getting worked up and pissed off at her for keeping
him away from the basement. He comes in after wandering
around for the last two hours, and when he finds out that
while he was gone an injured cat broke into the apartment
and that she'd had to literally sweep it out the back door, all
he can think about is how long he has to act like he gives a
shit before he can go back downstairs. James only wants to
be down in the basement. He resents most of the time he
spends upstairs, and he clearly believes that Mary is forever
oppressing him with things like the cat incident. But it isn't
James who is being oppressed by living with Mary, it's Mary
who is being oppressed by James. He thinks that living with
Mary distracts him from his life's work, when it is actually
Mary who is literally suffocated by their living arrangement. And maybe the biggest joke of all is that James thinks

that Mary is constantly making demands of him and his precious time when it is James who insists that every moment of their day be devoted in one way or another to his basement work. Mary is ashamed by how much of her life revolves around his ridiculous schedule. Especially now that they have to keep up such a regular sex routine. It bothers her the way she has to monitor his moods, waiting for the moment when he's least likely to be annoyed to suggest they go to the bedroom. 'If there was a way,' she would say, 'I'd be happy to leave you out of it.' And she meant it. The way he carried on made her feel almost guilty, as if she should feel grateful that he was willing to do his part. She hates herself for it, but she's even got into the habit of saying 'thank you.' And what's worse is that he smiles and nods, as if to say, 'You're welcome.' Why is it, if he wants a child as much as she does, that she feels like she is asking him for a favour? Why does he make it so she has to ask every time? He knows the schedule. They might have even talked about it earlier in the day or the night before, since it is increasingly common for her to give him a few gentle reminders so he won't feel like she is springing it on him out of the blue. 'Don't forget that we have to do it later,' she says. And then later on she might say something like, 'Is now a good time?' And he would nod and smile and basically carry on in the same way that her dad used to when doling out money during family trips to the amusement park, peeling off a couple bills with a lordly flourish but never enough that she wouldn't have to come back in an hour asking for more. So here she is at the kitchen table, staring at his back as he leans over the railing, the cat's blood drying out on the floor, while all she can think about is whether or not they'll be having sex tonight. Much like when they first started seeing each other, she obsesses a lot about when the next time will be, but the difference now of course is the total absence of desire. 'It's weird,' she thinks, 'to really want to have sex, without really wanting to have sex.' But this is what has happened to a lot of things in their life together – where they seem to be going through all the old motions with none of the old feeling. She really wants to buy their own place, not because she has strong opinions about handling their finances, or because she is eager to control her own property, but because this is what many of her friends are doing and she is anxious that they are falling behind. She worries that this approach even applies to wanting a family, that she doesn't want a child for *the right reasons*. 'What if I'm doing this out of a sense of obligation or duty,' she thinks, 'when maybe I don't even really want to have a family?' How can she even tell the difference between what she wants and what she thinks she wants? For instance, when dinnertime rolls around there's always a part of her that wants to scrap the home-cooked meal and just pick up some sushi. But whenever she does go through with it she never ends up enjoying it. She wishes she had stuck with the home-cooked meal because – she realizes, only after eating the cold and tasteless fish – that she actually doesn't like sushi, she just thinks she does. Mary sits at the kitchen table and watches James as he leans over the railing and pretends to look for the cat. Not only is he putting on an act so he can have a moment to himself, but he's also going through the motions so he can prove to himself and to her that he's done the right thing. Ridiculous. She gets up from the kitchen table and goes out to join him at the railing, both of them now staring into the gloomy alleyway, pretending to look for the cat. So much of their time is spent pretending for each other. She knows that when James is in the basement, he isn't really working away on one of his little projects. He is just hanging out downstairs so she'll think he's doing something meaningful and important. When James comes up and asks her what she's been up to she doesn't tell him she's been reading about infertility online. Instead she says something along the lines of 'not much' or 'nothing.' What's truly depressing is that none of this pretending actually works, or at least not the way it's supposed to, because neither of them is able to pull it off. 'But,' Mary thinks, 'that isn't really the point, is it?' When James asked her what she was up to after she'd just spent hours poring over medical websites, and she said, 'nothing,' she didn't expect that he'd take what she said literally. By pretending, she was telling him she didn't want to talk about it, it wasn't any of his business, and since there's so much these days that fit into these two categories she spends a lot of time pretending. 'What's the point?' Mary would think. 'It's not like there's anything we can do about it. So why bother talking about it?' The thought of talking about it makes her cringe. If, when James asked her 'what's up?' she were to tell him what was bothering her, why she spent so much time online looking at pictures of her friends, or reading up on infertility statistics, then he would try to comfort her, tell her to relax, be patient, try to live in the moment, and she knew that she wouldn't be able to stand it. She doesn't want to be comforted, to look on the bright side, count her blessings, and anything that would remind her, in ways that make her crazy, that she doesn't care about all the stuff she should be thankful for, she only cares about the thing she can't be thankful for. Who gives a fuck about blessings when the only thing you really want is never going to happen for you? She looks at James and guesses at what he might be thinking, probably wondering how long he has to pretend to care about the cat before he can go back down to the basement. Or maybe he really is bothered by the thought of the poor little thing suffering somewhere down there in the alley. It is impossible to tell. She considers asking him. All of a sudden she feels a profound need to know, as if their future depends on it. But just then the doorbell rings. For some reason, which, when she recalls it days later makes her wince with embarrassment, her initial thought is that it must be the police. 'Maybe they were close by when it happened?' she thinks. 'Maybe they heard something. . . .' A sickening feeling comes over her as she gradually realizes what a strange thought this is. What does she mean by 'when it happened'? Is she referring to when the cat was hit by the car? Or when she flung it against the kitchen table with the broom? In either case, just how stupid do you have to be to think that the police would investigate an injured cat? 'I don't really believe the police are at the door,' she thinks. But, just like when she saw the thing in the cat's jaws and thought it was a mouse, it was just the first thing that came to mind. James is also frozen in place because he is afraid of who might be at the door, but in his case he is almost certain that it is the con man. Horrified, he realizes that he must've been followed. Once he'd handed over the four hundred bucks the shame and humiliation had overcome him with such wearying force that he wandered the streets aimlessly while muttering 'You fucking idiot' over and over to himself, at first with disgust, then mellowing to anguished hopelessness. 'How is it possible,' he eventually asked himself, once he finally broke off from the *fucking idiot* mantra, 'when you knew right away that he wasn't for real, that you could even think for one second that he was telling the truth? And if you knew he was lying, why did you go to the bank machine?' As he asked himself these questions he kept replaying what had just happened, but it was as though it had already been obscured, or covered up, as if he'd managed to repress something that had taken place only moments ago. Yet he still saw enough to feel ashamed, since it seemed to him that instead of the naive faith he'd initially assumed had been the reason he was taken in by the con man, he'd actually just been scared. There was nothing quixotic behind the con, no foolish yet noble impulse inspired his willing blindness, it wasn't even that he'd been afraid that the con man was going to beat him up, nothing so specific, there was just a vague fear that somehow it wasn't going to turn out well, it was this, and nothing else, that made him hand over the four hundred dollars. 'You're a coward,' he said to himself, 'simple as that.' The elaborate rationale he'd gone through while he was getting conned was just that, an elaboration, the real truth was much simpler. 'You invent all this complex bullshit in order to hide the fact that everything you do, you do out of fear,' he thought. Adrift in his neighborhood he felt that he finally understood himself. He saw all his actions through the lens of this devastating realization. 'How could I have missed this before,' he asked himself, 'when it's so painfully obvious?' The horror of his behaviour spread out before him like an enormous tapestry or mural, where he could take his time and examine every instance of weakness in his past, and the scenes of the most abject fear and cowardice took place in the basement. He saw himself down there, alone, and in almost every sense of the word, lost. He'd thought that his life's work, however futile, had been an act of courage, when all along he'd been acting from the most banal and everyday anxieties. But just as he was punishing himself with these thoughts he experienced a sense of exhilarating possibility. 'It's not too late to change,' he thought. 'It's good that this happened. Otherwise I may have gone on like this indefinitely. Now I know what I need to do. Now I know what has been standing in my way.' He'd hurried home, hoping to put his epiphany to work right away, but Mary's cat incident had distracted him, so it was only now, as he is standing on the balcony after the doorbell had just rung, that all of this came back to him. 'You're afraid,' he says to himself. Although maybe he's right to be afraid? He'd been so distracted with his own thoughts while he was out wandering the streets that it had never occurred to him to check if he was being followed. He'd been so ashamed, once he'd handed over the four hundred dollars, that he'd wanted to put as much distance between himself and the con man as possible, short of breaking into a full sprint. Once he knew which way the con man was going, James told him that he lived in the opposite direction, but he hadn't waited to see which way the con man went. There was more than a little superstition to this behaviour, like the way a child runs away from a dark basement, terrified that if they turn around all the wild phantasms of their imagination will come to life – 'so,' he thinks as he stands next to Mary on the patio, with the faint reverberations of the doorbell still sounding through the apartment, 'it's more than possible that as he fled down the street the con man decided to wait and see where I went. And once I went far enough,' he thinks, 'he probably decided to follow me to see where I lived.' James had already revealed himself to be gullible and cowardly, so the con man probably figured it wouldn't be a bad idea to find out where he lived in case he wanted to hit him up later on. The entire time that James was wandering the neighborhood, lost in thought, the con man had been keeping a safe distance. James had thought that handing over the four hundred dollars was a stupid and reckless thing to do, but it turns out that he'd done something much much worse. Instead of putting distance between himself and the con man he has brought him even closer. In fact, it was this precise behaviour – to get as far away as he could and never look back – that turned what had been an embarrassing and inconvenient incident into something truly dangerous for himself and Mary. The entire time he'd been with the con man he never thought that the incident might end violently. Of all the possible scenarios that ran through his head as he tried to decide whether the stranger was *for real* or not, he never considered that he might be capable of the horrific sort of crimes that James had only ever read or heard about. It just wasn't on his radar. For all his introspection and deep thinking, he actually had a limited imagination. Far from being a free thinker, he was constrained by a host of blind spots and prejudices that reduced his realm of possibility down to a little set of expected outcomes, and anything that lay outside of this was almost impossible for him to see. He knows that, in principle, and in reality, all sorts of strange and wonderful things happen every day, and that it is technically possible for something unusual to happen to him, but as far as he knows, nothing ever has, and while he knew it is entirely possible that some day he could be surprised by an event so horrific and shocking that people might even read or hear about it, he felt it was just as likely that he'd become rich and famous, or discover that he has a long-lost twin brother. These things could *technically* happen, but they won't, at least not to him, so when he's walking with a stranger who he doesn't trust and may even be trying to con him out of four hundred dollars, he never suspects that the man has something much worse in mind, though it's completely feasible that the stranger's attempt to rip him off was only the first move in a more elaborate and sinister plot. The trick was to get James thinking that the *worst possible scenario* was that the stranger was lying to him about getting his car towed, when what the stranger might actually have been doing was sizing James up, figuring out whether he was a suitable victim or not. While James was distracted by the issue of four hundred dollars the stranger was thinking about how he was going to follow him back to his apartment and then torture and kill him and his wife. 'That's crazy,' James thinks as he stands completely still against the wall. And besides, that sort of thing doesn't happen nearly as much as we think it does. It's only because it's so gruesome and terrifying that we end up reading about this sort of thing. The proportion of people who die from being tortured by a total stranger is so tiny that you're probably more likely to get hit by a falling piano. We read about a couple who, while hiking across a foreign country, is slaughtered in their tent, the wife gang-raped and the husband brutally disfigured, and we think to ourselves, 'Good God! How awful. . . .' Then we read about someone who came from obscurity and became so rich and famous that they changed the shape of the world we live in, and we think to ourselves. 'Jesus Christ. That's amazing!' But we never think as we're reading about these horrible crimes that something similar might be in store for us. We never think, 'I suppose it's only a matter of time before my wife and I are murdered in the most extreme and unspeakable way.' But plenty of people say to themselves, 'Well, it's only a matter of time before I'm so rich and famous that I won't even be recognizable to myself.' The belief that if he kept going down to the basement (even if while he was down there he never got any work done, and on the rare occasion that he did occupy himself it was to undo the work of preceding weeks and months) and just put enough time in, regardless of his deficiencies of natural ability or acquired skill, he would eventually finish his life's work and create something of lasting value, somehow existed side by side with the belief that as long as he never did anything out of the ordinary he didn't have to worry about being one of those people you read or hear about and say to yourself, 'That's awful.' Except that, in the first case, he didn't actually believe that he had enough talent and skill to accomplish his goal, and that even if he had *all the time in the world* there was no way he'd ever complete his life's work, and despite all of this, he *still* has faith that somehow he will pull off something extraordinary and literally one of a kind, the sort of thing that only happens once every couple of centuries. Whereas, in the second case, he knows that even though it is statistically rare for someone to be tortured and killed, or to win the lottery, it is nevertheless something that happens all the time, and that these sorts of things (unlike creating or accomplishing a work of lasting value) are completely random and by definition can happen to anyone – it doesn't matter if you are normal because *that is who these things happen to*, someone has to be terrorized and killed, someone has to win the jackpot, these things have happened before, they will happen again, and they will continue to happen as long as there are people around to be tortured and killed, and even if you try to lower the odds by staying home or avoiding public transit, etc., it's still entirely possible that you will be tortured and killed in your own home. Even though it should have, it never crossed his mind (until now) that he might not have been dealing with a con man at all (at least not in the popular sense of the term), that he may in fact be a cold-blooded murderer, and that he was only pretending to con him out of four hundred dollars in order to keep him off balance and size him up. In the same way that someone who dies suddenly one night from a brain aneurysm comes home from work thinking they've got a stress headache, takes a couple Tylenol and goes to sleep, oblivious to what's coming (even though in hindsight it should have been obvious that instead of suffering from an ordinary headache they were dying from an extraordinary and statistically rare, but in another sense altogether ordinary brain aneurysm, and if they had only recognized what was really happening they may have gotten to the hospital in time to save their life, but instead condemned themselves to death by taking Tylenol and going to sleep) – in the same way, James did everything possible to make himself the ideal murder candidate. When the stranger first hailed him in the street James should have looked the other way and kept walking, and when the stranger started talking to him he should have pretended that he couldn't hear him. If he'd only indicated that he wasn't open to being approached or spoken to by a stranger – that, like most people, he was hostile to this sort of encounter – then the stranger would've decided that to try to open him up and gain his trust and then follow him home to murder him and his wife would be much too difficult, if not impossible. James could have said, 'No thanks,' or 'Not interested,' or even 'Go fuck yourself,' or he could have shook his head 'no' and kept on walking. His first reaction is always to say 'no,' to turn things down, to deny. If a friend asks him out for a drink, or invites Mary and him over for dinner, he has to fight the initial reflex of making up an excuse. An opportunity at work comes up and he has to force himself to apply, and if they ever did offer him a promotion he'd probably pass on it. All of this is a way of saying 'no' to life, of shutting things down so he's only doing the bare minimum, this way nothing can touch him, and because he has to devote so much of his life to his life's work, this saying 'no' to life is a way of making sure he'll have the time and energy to accomplish his goal. But every once in a while he is overcome with a desire to say 'yes' to life, and this, he thinks, is why he'd been open to the approach of a stranger, even though everything about the way that he was approached told James that the stranger wanted something and that he might be dangerous, or at least annoying. Because he is always turning things down or shutting them out he can sometimes become suddenly desperate to say 'yes' to life, and for life to say 'yes' back. This is what made him reckless, and it was why he was willing to hear what the stranger had to say. 'Maybe he really needs my help?' he had thought. This was how he ended up distracted by what he considered to be the problem of these sorts of encounters, which was whether to believe what the stranger was telling him, and not by the possibility that the con man might be a serious threat to his life, and not just the metaphorical life that James wanted to say 'yes' to. If he hadn't been so preoccupied with his own response then he may have had a completely different take on the encounter, he may have noticed something about the way the stranger was acting that would've indicated that he was actually a violent murderer, but instead he interpreted everything the stranger did or said only in the context of whether he was telling the truth about the money order. He had been in despair over whether the stranger was a con man when he should have been in despair over whether the stranger was a homicidal maniac, and even though these forms of despair were in some ways equal, the second form was much much worse, and he felt ashamed for only experiencing it once the doorbell started ringing. When he looks over at Mary he sees that her eyes are wide and he wonders if the reason she looks so apprehensive and frightened is because she can somehow sense what he's thinking. 'Who could it be?' she says, but before he can think of something to say she asks, 'Do you think it's the cops?' This question stuns him, because initially he sees it as confirmation that she knows everything that happened with the con man. Her fear that the police were at the door is similar to his fear that the con man followed him home, and so even though it is completely insane for him to think it, there is a moment when he feels like Mary is *reading his mind*. But then he realizes that she's talking about the cat incident. 'I know it's completely insane,' she whispers, 'but just when the doorbell rang I had a vision that it was the police here about the cat.' And just as she says this, the doorbell rings again. They stare at each other with the same bulging eyes and for a moment they stand there, hardly breathing. James is having a mild panic attack as he desperately tries to convince himself that he wasn't followed, while Mary, although certain that she is being completely irrational, is convinced that somehow *everybody knows what happened,* and that whoever it is on the other side of the door has come to tell her that they saw what she did. She mouths the words 'what do we do?' and James holds his finger to his lips, shushing her when she hasn't even made a sound. He motions for her to follow him into the kitchen and then pulls her up next to him where he is standing in front of the sink. They stare at the light from the hallway that is reaching across the kitchen floor, waiting to see if a shadow will pass over it and start to stretch across the threshold, as if the person (or persons) on the other side of the door might let themselves in and make their way towards them. The doorbell rings again and James flinches and grabs hold of Mary's arm, obviously afraid that she'll lose her nerve and decide to answer the door. He pulls her closer to him and shuffles along the counter so that eventually they are huddled in the space between the wall and the fridge. Mary pulls free and shoots him a look to let him know that he has nothing to worry about, that she is just as determined as he is to wait out this doorbell onslaught, no matter how long it takes. Despite how terrified he is that the stranger has come for them and that in a few moments they might be murdered in the same gruesome fashion that often captures the popular imagination and makes the rounds with all the major news media, he is moved by their silent pact and the way that they are hiding like a couple of fugitives waiting for the secret police to pass them by, or like a couple of kids who wander too far from home and get stuck in a storm, forced to wait it out, clutching each other and shuddering in the corner of an abandoned barn or under the wind-lashed branches of a massive tree. All of a sudden he wants to tell her about the stranger but the doorbell sounds again. Immediately the giddiness they were feeling is swept away and they stare intensely at each other, and wait for the echo of the chime to fade. While Mary is still terrified, a creeping sense of annoyance starts to come over her. 'If it was the police,' she thinks, 'they would've knocked by now, or something.' Whoever is at the door, however insistent they are being, they're also being polite, allowing for a long interval before pressing the doorbell each time. They clearly know we're home,' she thinks, 'or they think we're home – why else would they keep ringing? – but they're still being respectful about how late it is.' The doorbell sounds reticent, as if the person ringing it isn't sure of the address, or of what they are going to say if someone answers the door. Mary's annoyance turns to anger as she thinks about this shy, polite person ringing their doorbell at midnight on a Thursday. 'What the fuck do they want?' she says to herself. 'Can't they tell that even if we're home, we're not going to answer the door?' She no longer thinks that the person at the front door has anything to do with the cat incident. 'It's just some drunk idiot,' she thinks, 'who got lost and thinks

they're at their friend's place, or their girlfriend's.' It occasionally happens in their neighborhood. There's a universi-
ty nearby, so sometimes one of the drunk students will get
confused, knocking on the doors of apartments that they
mistakenly believe to be those of their friends, or friends of
friends, or their boyfriends, or maybe someone they met
earlier in the evening who played a mean trick and gave
them a bogus address. 'I can't fucking believe these kids,'
she thinks, and then, all at once she decides to answer the
door and confront the drunk student or students who were
ringing their doorbell in the middle of the night. As she
turns towards the hallway, James grabs her so fiercely that
she is overcome with fear all over again. He looks at her
with total panic in his eyes and she wonders if he knows
something she doesn't. 'What is it?' she mouths silently,
but he holds his finger to his lips and shoots her a look as if
she's been shouting at the top of her voice. They hold this
position – Mary staring at James questioningly while he
looks back with a crazed and panicked look in his eyes –
but after what must've been at least five minutes of complete silence it is obvious that whoever has been ringing the
doorbell has stopped. Mary asks, sarcastically, if it's safe to
talk, but James holds up his hand to silence her and then
disappears down the hallway. He comes back and nods and
tells her it's safe and she rolls her eyes and then asks him if
he's going to tell her what's going on. 'What do you mean?'
he says. 'You were being paranoid too. Just as much as me.'
'Yeah, but I know why I'm freaked out. I just bounced a cat
off our kitchen table, that then ran out of our apartment,

probably with its brains leaking out of its nose,' she is whisper-yelling (more yell than whisper), 'so I know why I'm freaking out, and even though it doesn't make any sense, and is probably only 'cause I feel guilty, I thought that maybe it was someone who saw the cat come though our window. Oh, God,' she gasps and grabs James's hand. 'What if it was the owner?' It is suddenly so clear to her that she is literally amazed that it wasn't the first thing she thought of. Obviously the cat escaped, or maybe it's just that he never stays out for long or strays very far from his home, so the owner is going around the neighborhood looking for it. Why else would somebody be ringing people's doorbells in the middle of the night? 'We should have answered the door,' she says. 'Why didn't we answer the door?' she looks at James with suspicion. 'What is going on?' 'Nothing,' James says. 'Nothing is going on. I was just thinking about what you said about it being the owner, which, no offense, is even more unlikely than the cops coming to our door. Even if it wasn't a stray, and chances are that it was, then it's not like the owner is going around ringing people's doorbells after the cat's only been gone for a short while. In fact,' he says, 'chances are they don't even know it's missing. If there even is an owner, that is.' But he can tell that he's not being very convincing, and even if he were, Mary was past the point of being convinced. Besides, he would feel so much better if he just told her about the stranger. He is always keeping things from her, holding back, hiding and dissembling, and it would be such an enormous relief to just let go, like one of those movie villains who is hanging on for *dear life* to the ledge of a tall building, or the hook of a towering construction crane. Maybe the hero is there too, holding onto the villain's sleeve (which is coming apart at the seam) or is slowly losing a grip on his hand, but at some point the villain realizes that it's useless, he is definitely going to fall, and the effort to keep dangling from the skyscraper or the construction crane is actually prolonging his agony – in fact, were he to resign himself to his fate and simply give in (i.e. to gravity/fate), then he may even find a sense of peace before hitting the ground. Just like this villain, who may have been a friend of the hero earlier in the movie and only now, at the precipice, is revealed to be an evil person, James is ready to let go. So he sighs and says, 'I'm worried that somebody followed me home.' As soon as he says this he regrets it. There's a swirl of emotions happening on Mary's face. Worry over what he may have done. Fear of what may still happen. Resignation that what's done is done and whatever may have happened, there's probably nothing she can do about it. Disgust, obviously, and love, which comes across like tender, if a little irritated, concern. But most of all there is a desperate need to know. When he kept things from her, it was as if he kept her in a state of *sensory deprivation*. When he lied to her, it always felt, when she eventually found out, like she'd been watching a movie or reading a book, and had fallen asleep or dropped into a lucid state, so the film or book got mixed up and blended into her thoughts and at some point, her memories as well, to the extent that years later, or maybe only days, she may recount a scene from that movie or book and tell it as if she were the hero of the story, without realizing that the story she was telling wasn't real. When she finds out he's been hiding something, or when he admits he's been lying to her, it's like realizing that certain memories you thought were yours are in fact made up and what you thought had happened hadn't actually happened at all. This is why she's so desperate to know – to know immediately what had happened – because now she knows that every memory is possibly tainted and until she knows which ones are real and which are made up, she can't be sure how to *respond*. But why does she need to wait and find out the specifics when she already knows the basics? It won't matter what James tells her, whether it is an enormous deception or only a minor incident, because what is revealed every time he admits to keeping something from her or deliberately misleading her, and in essence lying right to her face, is that she can't believe a word he says. There are practical considerations, of course. For example if, when they started seeing each other, James had concealed the full extent of his sexual history (which he had), and even exaggerated by a number of years when he'd last been checked for sexually transmitted infections (ditto), only to reveal the truth later on, in a guilty and irritatingly coy manner, clearly more apprehensive about how angry she would be than whether or not he'd passed on an STI, then she would be obliged to get tested and to insist that he get tested as well (which she did) and maybe even to insist that they get in the habit of getting tested regularly (which she didn't) since he obviously didn't take the whole STI thing very seriously, and if he did end up cheating on her some day (that is, if he hadn't already, or wasn't currently) then she couldn't rely on him to have the courtesy to use protection, or the balls to tell her if he hadn't. So even though, in the most general sense, it doesn't matter what James tells her, in another, more particular sense, so long as she continues to live with him, and love him, and try to have a baby with him, everything that he says, and all that he doesn't, may be immediately and even disastrously significant. She can't afford to be philosophical about his pathological dishonesty. It isn't an option for her to say to herself, 'Everything he says or doesn't say is misleading, so by definition I can't believe a word that comes out of his mouth. All I can do is trust my instincts. He lies about some things so all things are potentially lies, and there is no way for me to know what is legit.' It would have been convenient to adopt this radical philosophical position, but the reality of the situation – the real reality – was that even though she couldn't, she had to trust him when he told her something, and if he was silent she had to trust that this was because he didn't have anything to say. Her dilemma is exacerbated by the fact that, from what she can tell, there is no method or rationale behind what he decides to be dishonest about. About a year ago, as an experiment, she decided to test how often he lied to her about what he looked at online. She didn't pick this as a test because of any concern on her part over his online behaviour, but it occurred to her that because the computer kept a record of every website he visited it would be easy to confirm the truth of what he told her. She started off with something easy. She knew he jerked off to porn. It wasn't an *issue* for them. They didn't fight about it. And for the most part he was discreet about it, so she didn't have to suffer the indignity of catching him in the act. But every once in a while he would get sloppy and leave a window open on a porn site. This had only happened a couple of times, and after she brought it up with him, it never happened again. The first time he slipped up was a turn-off, but she tried to overlook it. She'd seen porn before, but even though the internet was supposedly drowning in it, she never really noticed it, and definitely didn't seek it out. Not because she had anything against it, it simply had no appeal for her. The one time she actually made an attempt to watch it and masturbate, she had to shut it off because she kept rolling her eyes, it was all so embarrassing, so ridiculously fake, and she didn't find it sexy at all. But when she woke up one Saturday morning after they had been drinking with Tim and Ellen (she went to bed the second they got in, while he stayed up to 'have a snack'), she found the browser open to a paused clip of a girl getting fucked in the back of a cab by two guys. In this new context (watching the porn that James had been jerking off to the night before), she was much more troubled by what she saw. The girl was so *tiny*. She couldn't have been older than twenty, and the guys that were fucking her were so big, literally covered in muscles, with gigantic cocks, and they were fucking her *so hard*, in a kind of frenzy, and the fact that they were in the back of a moving cab, instead of seeming erotic and risqué, struck her as extremely bizarre.

/ 165

The video was like a form of insanity, but still she wasn`t offended so much as disturbed by how incongruous the on-screen scene was with what she and James did when they fucked, or made love, or whatever. 'If this is what he likes to watch on his own,' she thought, 'then what is going on in his head when we're doing it?' These thoughts bothered her for a couple of days, but eventually the memory of the scene in the taxi lost its visceral and disturbing quality, and she even felt a bit foolish for getting worked up over something that was completely harmless and probably just a way of blowing off steam. Besides, literally millions of people watched porn, so how could there be something wrong with it? The next time he forgot to close the browser after he'd been jerking off the night before, she wasn't disturbed like the first time, only disgusted, the way she got when he forgot to flush after taking a shit, so she didn't think anything of asking him when they were on the couch together later that morning if he could try to remember to close down his porn sites when he was done with them. He didn't reply and looked so terrified that she felt as though she needed to reassure him. 'I don't mind,' she explained. 'I get it. Well, I don't really get it. But I know it's natural, or at least it's pretty fucking common, so I don't think it's weird. Although, do you always watch that extreme shit?' James was about to reply but she cut him off. 'Never mind, watch whatever you like, I mean, how often do you look at it?' 'Hardly ever,' he said. 'Just, you know, once in a while, when I feel like blowing off some steam.' She couldn't help making a face at this, 'How can you blow off steam watching two steroid junkies fucking some teenager into oblivion?' But she cut him off again before he could reply, 'Never mind. Sorry. I really don't care. You don't have to defend yourself. Just please try to remember to close it down when you're done.' He promised that he would and they never talked about it again, except for when they got into a slump and she'd get suspicious that he was bingeing on porn, but even then all she would do is make a remark like, 'You're probably too tired from watching anorexic teenagers getting pounded by hairless Neanderthals.' And he'd make some lame attempt at a joke, like, 'That's racist.' But she knew that he was ashamed of his porn habit, so it was ideal for her *test* because he would almost certainly lie when she asked him about it. So one morning she woke up and snuck out to the computer to check its history. Sure enough, James had an epic jerk-off session the night before. From 1:43 a.m. to 2:27 a.m. he went through close to a dozen videos. She clicked on a few links to get a flavour for what he'd been watching, and was surprised to see that the first couple were fairly tame – a woman fingering herself poolside and another using a vibrator in the shower (*why the shower?*) – but a couple of the other links were more hardcore – a girl wearing a ball gag riding some sort of machine, and a Czech woman with gigantic tits getting fucked next to a dumpster while the man who was fucking her filmed it from his point of view with a cheap camcorder. Once again, she was disturbed by how the images onscreen were so *utterly foreign* to the sort of sex that she and James had. And now that she was actually tracking the specifics of his behaviour she

/ 167

wasn't able to dismiss it so easily. Forty-four minutes. That's how long he sat in front of the computer screen last night. How many nights every week? Every month? How many hundreds or thousands of minutes of this shit did he watch every year while she was asleep in their bed, or out doing groceries, or having drinks with her friends? *Of course* he would lie about watching all this porn. It was obscene. She crawled back into bed and lay there thinking, careful not to touch him, until he woke up. 'Were you watching porn last night?' she said, as soon as he opened his eyes. 'Well good morning to you too,' he said, with a sleepy grin on his face. 'Well, were you?' He draped his arm over her and she rolled it off. 'Um, did I leave something open?' he frowned, apologetically. 'What do you think?' He raised himself on his elbow, 'I think that you're upset that I look at porn, which I totally understand. It's just something I like to do to blow off steam after working in the basement. But if it bothers you I'll stop.' She'd expected him to lie, but she realized that she'd come on too strong and gave herself away. Now she was curious to see if he would come clean, or whether he'd try to hide the *extent* of his habit. 'So what? Like five minutes at the end of the night? A clip or two and then you come to bed?' 'Exactly,' he said, 'I'm not some sort of depraved pervert.' 'So last night you watched what? Five or ten minutes?' He lay back on the pillows and sighed, as if she'd already been questioning him for an hour and he'd answered this question many times, 'Yeah, something like that.' 'And what were you watching?' She was sitting straight up and studying him closely, trying to spot any tics or 'tells' so she could watch out for them during the next test. 'Jesus, Mary, I don't know. It's pretty normal stuff. Girls fingering themselves. That sort of thing.' 'So,' she leaned back, almost relaxed, 'you didn't watch videos of gagged women getting fucked by machines for forty-five minutes?' James got dressed in a rage, throwing the sort of tantrum that usually would've come off as comical, but, all things considered, was just kind of sad. They made up later that night, but Mary knew that from then on he would always be careful to wipe the computer's history. 'Or maybe,' she had thought, 'he might give it up.' Either way, she let it drop. She couldn't blame him for watching porn, or if she did there would be millions of other people she'd have to include in her blame, and she certainly couldn't blame him for lying about it when she had questioned him in a way that encouraged him to lie. For the next test she would pick something so banal that there would be no good reason to lie about it. Lying about watching porn – the type he watched, and how much – was predictable. These sorts of lies weren't the problem because she could anticipate them, which is to say that whether he lied or told the truth she'd be able to guess at what he was up to, and plan accordingly (like get tested for STIs, or make enough noise when she woke up to go to the bathroom that she wouldn't catch him masturbating). The bigger problem was that he might be lying about the most random details and events of his life, and that this randomness made it impossible to predict with any degree of certainty what was actually going on in their lives. What he ate for lunch? The last time he spoke with his parents? Whether he got any work done when he was down in the basement? There was nothing that he didn't try to distort. 'Did you get that link I sent you?' she would ask. 'I haven't checked my email yet today.' But when he'd go to the bathroom she would check the browser history and see that he'd already checked his email three times. Why would he lie about something that was so inconsequential? In what way could it matter to him whether or not she knew if he'd checked his email and seen the link that she had sent him? What exactly was it that he was concealing? It had just been a link to an article about a restaurant they had eaten at recently, one they didn't like. The reviewer praised the restaurant extravagantly, slavishly, and – in Mary's opinion – was clearly in awe of the celebrity chef and the ostentatious décor and pretentious menu. This was typical of the reviewer's previous articles, which had all been displays of cultural illiteracy. If a restaurant was a sham, an incoherent mishmash of styles and influences, then it would be praised for its originality, whereas a beautiful restaurant serving an eloquent cuisine composed with masterful simplicity would get panned for being uninspired or unoriginal, or both. So whenever they wanted to go out to eat she would check to see if this reviewer had written about the restaurant and she and James could tear the review apart. They would talk over dinner, or later as they sat on the couch, about the crass and inept similes, the overwrought and often incomprehensible prose, and they would both get so worked up and exasperated over what they perceived as an offense against good taste that they might even plan on starting a blog of their own to take revenge by posting comments made in the privacy of their living room that would be devastating to the reputation of the reviewer if they were ever made public. She liked how worked up James would get, though at times they got so worked up that they would start to argue, even when they were in complete agreement. She got excited at the idea that they might somehow develop these bitch sessions into something that other couples might read and talk about over dinner, or while they hung out with friends. But she wasn't delusional, she knew that they would never start a blog, that these high-strung responses to the reviewer were simply a way for them to sort out the confusion and envy they felt whenever their opinions were contradicted or refuted in the media, that it was a harmless pastime but in other ways crucial to their fragile intimacy, so even though it was bewildering for James to lie about checking his email, it was hurtful all the same, and she was determined to find out what it was he thought he was hiding. 'I did sign in,' he explained when she confronted him later over dinner, 'but I was waiting to hear back from Dale about next weekend. I saw that you had sent me something, but I didn't look at it.' 'But that's not what you said,' she said, thrown by this lawyerly horseshit. 'You said you hadn't checked your email when you'd already checked it three times.' 'Well, first of all,' he was speaking with the same tone of barely contained rage that he used whenever she challenged one of his lies, 'I'm still trying to understand why you're spying on my online activity. But I don't even know if I want to talk about that right now. Frankly, I don't know whether I should be offended, or concerned. But I guess I said it that way because I hadn't checked the email you sent me yet and I didn't want to have to explain to you that I was only checking to see if Dale had got back to me. I knew that if you knew that I had checked my email that you would want to know why I didn't check out the link that you sent me, and that you wouldn't leave me alone until I did, and I just didn't feel like reading a fucking review and then getting into one of our bitch sessions about how much of an idiot the reviewer is.' 'So it's my fault you lied?' she exclaimed, hurt by the way he described their conversations about the restaurant reviewer. 'Kind of,' he said. After this fight she noticed that he got into the habit of clearing the history on the laptop every time he used it. If she wanted to catch him in a lie after that she had to wait for him to slip up. As it happened, an opportunity came up only a few days later when Mary was emptying the recycling bin under the sink. She noticed a balled-up plastic bag as she was transferring the recycling into the blue bags. 'I use these for my lunches,' she said to herself (pissed at James for carelessly throwing out the bags that he knew she used for lunches). Besides, she thought to herself, were you even allowed to get rid of plastic bags like that (putting them in the recycling bin that is), even if the only alternative, which struck her as perverse, would be to throw them out? As she was putting the bag into the drawer full of plastic bags, she felt a piece of paper through the plastic – a receipt for takeout food from a restaurant that they had often talked about going to, but whenever the opportunity came up they bailed at the last minute, worried that the food wasn't going to be as good as what they had been led to expect from the reviews and their friends. 'People go crazy for that shit,' she would say, 'and it never ends up being as good as they make it out to be.' 'It's true,' James would agree, 'I don't know what it is about places like that but the moment people get inside they lose the ability to taste the difference between good food and total garbage.' It was the conviction in his voice that would convince her to play it safe and order from one of the takeout places that they trusted and had been using for years. Now, here he was, going to this new restaurant that all their friends had been talking about, and doing it behind her back. She stood at the kitchen sink, stunned with hurt, and tried to understand why he would want to go to the takeout place without her, why he preferred to have the experience all by himself even though trying out new restaurants was something they always did together, and, more importantly, why he wanted to hide it from her and keep her believing that this was still a place that they would try out one night when they finally stopped worrying over whether it was overrated? It was hurtful that he chose to go on his own but it was disturbing that he intended to keep her in the dark after the fact. What was he going to do when they eventually went there together? Was he going to pretend that it was his first time? She saw herself sitting there waiting for their order, talking about the menus, criticizing the counter setup, and there he would be, going along with it, agreeing with her suggestions and even saying that it might be a good idea to use one of those pagers that beeped when your table was ready so they wouldn't have to stay crammed in the doorway blocking the entrance. She experienced a falling feeling. Not as drastic as the horrific free fall in her dreams – more muted, but surprising, like missing the first step on a staircase. So she called down into the basement, something she was supposed to do only when *it absolutely couldn't wait*, and he came up the stairs with that look on his face. 'What's wrong?' he said. 'Did you go to that new takeout place without me?' She immediately regretted putting it to him like that. She should've been more casual about it. He might've slipped up and revealed the real reason for the cover-up, instead of spitting out the first lie that came into his head. 'Yeah,' he said, as if she'd just asked him something trivial that hardly justified breaking the rule about yelling down into the basement, 'I went to try it out that night you met Veronica for drinks.' She thought back to their conversation from that night. She was certain that she'd asked him what he'd had for dinner, but she couldn't remember what he'd said. 'Didn't I ask you what you ate when I got home?' 'If you had,' he said, 'then I would've told you that I got takeout.' 'But I thought we were going to go there together,' she was thrown off by her memory lapse and felt like she had to accept his reply, even though she had the feeling that he was full of shit. 'We always go to new places together. We had just been talking about going there last week. . . . Jesus,' she said after a sudden thought, 'have you gone there before? Or was this your first time?'

GIVING UP

'Holy shit,' he yelled. 'This is fucking ridiculous. It was my first time there. You were out. I felt like treating myself and I was bored with our usual places, so I went there. I'm sorry. We can order from there tomorrow if you want. Okay? Is the interrogation over now?' 'Yes,' she said. 'Fine.' But once he was back in the basement she obsessed over the night that she'd gone out for drinks with Veronica, and in particular what she had talked about with James when she got home. Maybe he wasn't lying. It's possible she hadn't asked him what he had for dinner, even though it is usually one of the first things she asked whenever they spent the night apart. She should've been more careful. Instead of asking up front if he'd been to the restaurant she could've worked up to it by mentioning that she was talking with a co-worker who'd gone the night before and wouldn't shut up about it all day, and then suggesting that they go there this weekend to finally see what everyone was talking about. She could've withheld the receipt and if he'd admitted to going a few nights ago then he'd never know that she had known. But if, worst-case scenario, he pretended at the restaurant that weekend that it was his first time there, she could bring it out, even though it made her sick that this is what she'd come to, catching him in a lie like some fucking TV lawyer. So because she forgot to be sneakier, he was able to get away with acting as if his trip to the new takeout place was of no significance, when in fact it signified everything that was wrong in their lives together. 'Next time,' she said to herself, 'I'll set things up so there will be none of this *he said/she said* horseshit. Either he'll be lying or telling the truth. None of this grey-area garbage.' Of course by now she knows that everything he says is a *potential lie*. If he went through the trouble of concealing something that was (in a certain sense) as insignificant and inconsequential as his trip to the new takeout restaurant (even though it was in another sense of major significance and dire consequence) then he must be lying and concealing all sorts of other banal facts about his life and events and people and basically everything that makes up a person's existence. It isn't the first time she has caught him lying about or trying to hide something that, when she found out what it was, struck her as so meaningless that she was at a complete loss as to why he would bother hiding it in the first place. At first, she saw these incidents the same way she did his occasional drinking binges (which came on without any warning and only happened once every year or so, when, out of the blue, he would get suddenly and spectacularly drunk for days, sometimes longer). The way that he would shift from having a good time with a few close friends over a couple of drinks to chugging back full glasses of whiskey and making a fool of himself was so out of character for him that she saw it as an aberration, like a freak storm, the sort of thing that is so rare and random that it's remembered for years afterwards as an alien event, the sort of thing that *never happens around here*, even though it did, and does. But as the number of lying incidents increased it became impossible to see his deceptions over petty events and details as something random, or *outside his normal behaviour*, when it was more than likely – this thought filled her with an intense anxiety – that this behaviour was systemic and deeply rooted. She used to think all this lying was maybe a temporary thing, that he'd eventually give it up and just be himself, but now she knows that the lying is his *true self*. And it isn't even the systemic lying that causes her creeping unease and even horror – what is really disturbing about all of this is that he is trying to conceal things about himself that she is perfectly aware of. No matter how many times he lies or withholds something, he never actually succeeds in hiding what it is he doesn't want her to see. In fact, it's the opposite, he reveals things about himself that she is aware of but that don't really bother her. Why go through so much trouble to keep things from her that were so ordinary? It was like a murderer who tries to defend himself by saying that he only meant to scare his victim. By trying to come up with an excuse, he makes everything worse. He is so worried that she might be upset with him for going behind her back and trying the new takeout restaurant without her that he doesn't even consider the implications of lying to her about something like that. 'I don't want you to know me,' he is saying to her. 'I don't want you to see me for who I really am. I want you to think I am something that I am not. Because what I am is someone who doesn't want to be what they really are. And what I really am is something much worse than what I appear to be.' Which is just a convoluted way of saying that all he really is, at the bottom of his heart, or at the end of the day, is what he doesn't want to be. And this, Mary suspects, is why he spends all his free time down in the basement pretending to work on something that both of them know he will never finish. He doesn't want to be who he really is, which is a mostly decent, sympathetic and altogether ordinary guy. He is terrified of the ordinary fate in store for him, the same fate that awaits millions of other people like him who lead quietly desperate lives that are by and large pleasantly uneventful. He is determined to escape the trap that he feels has been set for him since the moment he was born – to have just enough awareness to understand what he would never be capable of. The moment he set out on his life's work he knew that the whole thing was a sham. 'Here I am,' he thinks to himself more or less every time he has a glimmer of clarity, 'pretending to have faith in what I'm doing, when what I really believe I'm doing – instead of making incremental progress on my life's work – is ruining any chance of enjoying the normal life that is my true fate.' This is what his life's work really is, an elaborate denial of *what he really is.* So when he tells her that he thinks someone may have followed him home, what he's actually saying to her is, 'I don't want to pretend anymore. I don't want to hide. From this moment on I'll never lie or conceal anything from you ever again.' And he really believes this – that it's possible, after years of distorting every aspect of his character, to make a complete break from this behaviour and become the sort of person who is at peace with who he is, who claims to be nothing else, who manages to somehow be at once of the world and completely out of it, entirely oneself and at the same time no one at all, instead of continuing as someone who – to justify (or at least excuse) his life – tries to set himself apart by pursuing his life's work, but only ends up pretending to work toward this life-affirming goal, which, instead of setting him apart, confirms his place in the undistinguished mass of people who never *make anything of themselves*, and live their lives in regret. Maybe, until now, the only reason that he hasn't given up these ridiculous pretentions is on account of a persistent and by now borderline superstitious faith that even though it is clearly impossible to escape his perfectly ordinary, and therefore terrifying fate, he still believes it might happen somehow. So maybe instead of always trying to keep some distance from what he is, and what Mary thinks he is, he gives up on trying to control her perspective. 'I'll tell her everything that happened between me and the stranger, leave nothing out,' and just the thought of finally giving up so totally on the farce of the last decade of his life is so exhilarating that he starts to shake. So he tells her what happened when he took a break from his so-called life's work and went for a walk around the block. Even though he is only telling her about the encounter with the stranger, he feels as though he is confessing his innermost secrets, exposing everything that up until now he has kept hidden, basically because he was afraid of what they signified (i.e. the person he really is, instead of the person he thought he was). 'That's all over with now,' he thinks, 'Now I'm finally coming clean.' After keeping a distance from Mary for the last ten years – estranging himself – and refusing to acknowledge the very basis of their shared reality, he is all of a sudden in a hurry to close this gap, to obliterate this distance, so there would be nothing between them any longer, no obstruction between who he is and who she thought he was. He wants to tell her everything, not just about the stranger, but about his life's work and how he's been steadily destroying the little he has managed to accomplish, and about how he is relieved that she hasn't been able to get pregnant, even though he feels extremely guilty because he knows how devastating it is for her. He wants to tell her about the porn, his crazy money issues, all the lies, etc. He wants to tell her about the anguish he feels every day he goes to work, and how he's just been coasting along for years, but is starting to worry that he isn't going to be able to keep the act up for much longer. Most of all, he wants to confess to the absolute despair he feels whenever he is down in the basement and he stops to consider the mess that he's made of his life, how he has gradually and inexorably closed off every possibility until he's reduced himself to the singular goal of succeeding or failing at his life's work. He put off having a family because he thought it might distract him. He never seriously pursued a career since it would have got in the way of his true calling. He no longer has close friends and merely keeps up a few acquaintances to help fill out the scattered milestones he still bothers to commemorate. Family relations have dwindled down to holidays, a few tentative telephone conversations, and the odd, grudging visit. He has no other hobbies or enthusiasms, or even habits really, because every moment of his waking life is infected by his life's work. He'd made a bet, a colossal gamble. He'd gone *all in*. And increasingly he is convinced that it was a bad bet. He no longer believes in himself and his life's work and he is certain that instead of being the sort of person who struggles heroically in the face of ceaseless opposition, ignoring the pleas of their family and friends to listen to reason and give up their reckless and destructive pursuit, conquering the darkest moments of self-doubt, suffering through the most soul-sucking adversity and near-unbearable deprivations, only to ultimately triumph and prove everyone wrong by creating a work of enormous and lasting significance, he is actually the sort of person you never hear about or read about, who ends up wasting years of his life stubbornly ignoring the sensible advice of concerned loved ones, repressing the mounting suspicions that he has made a crucial mistake, that he should never have put any faith in his ability or talent, that instead of ultimately triumphing and proving everyone (including himself) wrong, all of his effort and sacrifice will amount to nothing, and he will end up disgraced and alone, tormented to the end of his days by thoughts of what he could have and should have done instead of devoting his life to a lost cause. All of this is racing through his mind as he tells Mary about his encounter with the con man, but instead of confessing these thoughts to her, he is giving an exhaustive account of the previous hour, describing the stranger's appearance (dishevelled *and* good-looking) and the street that they met on, what the stranger said and how he said it, what James said and what he was thinking about throughout the encounter. 'In order for her to understand why I did what I did,' he thinks, as he's describing the con

/ 181

man's facial hair, 'she has to know what was going through my mind.' He worries that she'll get hung up on the fact that he'd given away four hundred dollars to a complete stranger, and draw all sorts of misguided and cynical conclusions about why he fell for such an obvious and clichéd routine, the sort of scam that nobody, not even kids or old people, would fall for anymore. It's extremely important for him that she understand the *full context* behind what happened. He totally sympathizes with her. If he was in her place he'd have an equally hard time understanding how she could be so naive, and he might end up suspecting that she was keeping something from *him*, that she had been attracted to the stranger, maybe that she even went into an alley with him and in a moment of insane recklessness fucked him while hanging onto a chain-link fence, or leaning up against a red brick wall – why else would she hand over four hundred dollars to someone she just met unless she was hoping to profit in some way, whether it was an explicit exchange (i.e. money for sex) or something more ephemeral, such as the erotic charge from giving over such a large sum of money to a good-looking man who was potentially dangerous, but more likely just desperate and dishonest? It is simply inconceivable that she could be taken in by such a glaringly obvious con, so the only way she would fall for something like that is because she hoped to gain something, and that what she was hoping for was illicit, a betrayal that would no doubt be of a sexual nature. There is no way, if it had been Mary instead of James who had been so easily duped, that he wouldn't end up suspecting her of some form of infidelity, either actual or only potential. So he knew that the only way to deal with the suspicions that Mary would most certainly have was to make an exhaustive confession. If he explained his exact frame of mind leading up to his encounter with the con man, as well as his precise train of thought right up to the moment he handed over the four hundred dollars, then there would be no room for her doubts or anxieties or paranoid thoughts because she would be able to see that he had left nothing out. Even the most trivial and tangential digression would be included. This is the only way he could prevent her from getting the wrong idea. Only the most complete accounting of every thought that passed through his mind, every utterance, the tiniest gesture, would succeed in depicting what actually happened between James and the stranger, anything less than that would be a distortion, a misrepresentation, and a lie. 'Everything is relevant,' he thinks. 'Everything is significant.' There is no other way for Mary to understand what happened out there unless she has all the facts. People think they can get the gist of a situation if they are furnished with the outline of an event. 'Just give me the broad strokes,' they say, 'I can fill in the rest.' We think that we know what happened because we've seen it all before. One situation resembles the next, and there's nothing that can't be compared, and equated, with something that came before. 'The same thing happened to me,' we say in order to be spared the trouble of listening to a story or an excuse that we feel as though we've already heard a million times before. 'I know what happens next,' we say, because even as we claim to believe that each event is different, that every situation is unique, the reality is that there's nothing anybody can tell us that we haven't already heard in one version or another, at least a million times before. Mary sits there and listens impatiently as James recounts, in the most exhaustive detail possible, an anecdote that, although in literal terms is unique, and technically has never happened before, is nonetheless painfully familiar. She already knows, the moment he starts telling his story, what he is going to say and how it is going to end. His precise train of thought, the exact details of what he said and what he did, while absolutely fascinating to him, are so predictable that she would wince when she saw them building into a long, drawn-out story. What does it matter to her how he was feeling or what he was thinking when he handed over four hundred dollars to a complete stranger, if it's all the same in the end? The moment she hears him say, 'A really good-looking guy approached me on the street and asked me to cash a money order for him,' she immediately knows that the story will end with him falling for this obvious scam, so that everything else he says, all the details he thinks are so important, are, for her, beside the point. She doesn't see his confession in the same way he does. He thinks he is shining a bright light onto his life, but all she sees is an embarrassing attempt to cast a shadow over the central truth of his story. 'He's stalling,' she thinks. Instead of just coming out with it, he is trying to bury the truth under this endless preamble where he just keeps piling on the details, which, among friends, at parties, can sometimes be amusing, but at home, in a tense situation like this one, after she has just told him about the cat incident, is the sort of thing that would make her furiously impatient. But she knows if she tries to cut him off and force him to skip to the end, to *get to the point* and stop trying to conceal what it is he did behind some complex rationale that's impossible to understand anyway and does nothing to change the fact that he probably got conned out of four hundred dollars, she would only be prolonging his little act and he'd end up heaping on even more needless detail, because, in his words, he got the 'impression that she didn't understand what he was trying to tell her.' 'No,' he would say, 'it's not like that at all,' and then he would go off on some weird tangent that wouldn't change her impression of the situation in the least, except to piss her off for being forced to sit and listen to even more horseshit. But once James has started on one of his explanations, it is impossible to convince him that he is wasting his time, that nothing he says will make a difference and that, if anything, instead of giving her a more nuanced and sympathetic perspective on what happened, it will end up making her more upset than if he had laid everything out at the start. Why couldn't he face up to the reality of the situation? Why did he think that he could somehow end up with an alternate reality, as if he could talk his way into another world? She is sitting and listening to James as he is going on about forging triplicate forms, when a feeling of hopelessness starts to take over. How many times have they sat on that couch, just as they were doing now, while James tried to explain the world away? If he forgot to pick up groceries after he promised he would, then she would be forced to listen to him explain why, instead of being thoughtless and annoying, he was actually *too thoughtful*, and by overthinking what he should pick up for dinner he ended up getting distracted, and before he realized what had happened he was back at the apartment, empty-handed. Or, when James made a bizarre and hurtful remark about Mary's body during a dinner with Veronica and her new boyfriend, once they got back home and Mary confronted him, she would have to sit and listen as he told her that what she thought was criticism was in fact a type of ironic praise. Far from trying to humiliate her in front of her friends, he had wanted to put her at ease, since he knew that she was sensitive about the little bit of weight she'd put on in the last year. Nothing is what she thinks it is, everything is the opposite of what it appears to be. He never let her have her own thoughts and constantly forces her to adopt his. It doesn't matter what her perspective is, he won't leave her alone until she sees things the way he sees them. By now she is so used to this that she's got in to the habit of keeping her thoughts to herself so he doesn't try to change them. This is why she doesn't interrupt him while he tells the story of his encounter with the stranger, because if he suspects that she doesn't wholeheartedly believe everything he tells her, then he'll keep heaping on more and more examples and excuses until he's satisfied that she's given up her own opinions and taken on his instead. 'Even though I knew he was full of shit,' James says, 'part of me was almost desperate to believe what he was telling me. Do you know what I mean?' She nods, yes, she knows exactly what he means, while she thinks to herself, 'What the fuck is he talking about? Why the hell would he want to believe the story of some sketchy guy off the street? What did it matter to him if the guy was lying?' It seems to her that it would've been better if the guy *had* been full of shit, because then it would've been easier to refuse to help him out. If it had been her, and she'd thought the guy was telling the truth, then she may have felt bad about it, but she still wouldn't have handed over four hundred dollars. From what she can tell, James is saying he never really doubted that the guy was a con artist. 'I thought that maybe he just seemed like a con man because that was the most obvious possibility,' he explains. 'Like it was such a cliché – from out of town, car trouble, a money order that he can't cash, if I could spare a couple minutes I'd be a hundred dollars richer for my trouble – everything about it was so pathetically obvious that I started to think he must be telling the truth. Otherwise he would've come up with something more plausible. Does that make any sense?' 'Of course it does,' she says, even though she is thinking that he must be out of his mind. This is the man she is trying to have a baby with? This naive and reckless fool? How could she have ever thought that this was the right thing to do? How had she missed so much about him? His impracticality? His profound gullibility? This destructive insecurity? Maybe he hadn't always been like this? Maybe he used to be stronger, clear-sighted, level-headed, simple. But this isn't the case. It had all been there at the beginning, she just hadn't seen it for what it was. She used to listen to him talk for hours about his life's work, happy to sit there as he explained what he was working on and hoping to finish *before too long* – it had been early in their relationship, and she was secretly proud to be going out with someone who had a calling and devoted his life to accomplishing something grandiose. Without thinking about what actually lay in store for her, she would even fantasize about what it would be like to be famous one day. Even if he wasn't very successful, she would think, eventually he was bound to be recognized. It wasn't that he seemed particularly brilliant that made her think this – she could tell that he was smart, but there were loads of smart people out there. It was that he was so obsessed with the goal of accomplishing something original and relevant and significant that he ended up convincing her he was capable of it. *Somebody* has to devote themselves to great works, she would say to herself, why not him? 'Genius is one percent inspiration and ninety-nine percent perspiration,' her dad used to say. If James is willing to devote himself to working non-stop on some monumental project that most people don't even bother attempting, let alone actually pull off, then he must have that one percent of inspiration that her dad was so dismissive of, and as long as he was willing to do the perspiration thing then he might even succeed. She had never been with someone who talked so much about some far-off and likely fanciful day in the future when he will have done something truly great and all that work will have finally paid off and he'll be recognized for his singular genius. It's undeniably exciting, when you're young, to sit and listen to someone talk about how, through the force of their own will, they will shape the world around them. 'Don't worry about how things look right now,' they say, 'because once I'm finished everything will have changed for the better. We may be struggling to pay our rent and bills while our friends are getting rich and moving into luxury condos and nice suburban homes, and we may spend most of our time fighting over the most mundane crap, something in the news, or the exact itinerary of a trip to France we took five years ago, there may be nothing about me that would lead you to believe that I'm destined for great things – in fact, everything you know about me would discourage great expectations of any kind – but if you just hang on and put all your trust in me, if you invest everything you have to give, then I promise you that one day all of this will change,' they say. 'Your faith in me will be redeemed and I promise that you'll even be rewarded for your *loyalty*. We will have a life that is the exact opposite of the one we are presently living. Instead of aimlessly wandering through each day and blindly going through the motions our lives will be filled with purpose and meaning. Instead of obligations, you will have goals. In fact,' they claim, 'it may not feel like it, but everything you are doing right now is infused with this higher purpose. When you do the groceries it only feels like a chore, but what you are actually doing is fulfilling an essential role in the great pursuit of my life's work. It may seem like getting into a desperate argument over how to spend the tax return is just another trial in the unending drudgery of our monotonous lives, but what you are actually doing is supporting an essential aspect of the process that will result in a monumental accomplishment.' It's with this sort of talk that James would try to convince Mary that, although their friends were better off in the form of really nice apartments and houses, as well as frequent vacations and nights out to nice restaurants, their lives were in many ways much less rewarding than they actually seemed. And sometimes she even believed him. But she eventually developed a bunch of nagging doubts that she couldn't reconcile with this vision of some glorious future. For starters, James's day job is completely unrelated to his life's work. At first this hadn't bothered her, it even reassured her, since, according to James's reverse logic, it confirmed his *outsider status*. 'Outsiders,' he would say, 'always find a way in. That's what makes them outsiders.' When he talked like that it *did* bother her, because without any outside confirmation of the validity of his life's work, all she had to go on was his ability to convince her, and that seemed to be weakening over the years. She also got the impression that he had given up, and in some ways that's what bothered her the most. It felt like a betrayal, or at least a mean trick. She felt the same sort of swelling anger she experienced whenever he got them lost on one of their vacations or camping trips. He always wanted to find the route that nobody else took, or the place that nobody went to see, the hard-to-find, out-of-the-way, exclusive spots he felt would distinguish them from the endless stream of tourists that passed through these locales. 'We don't want to go there,' he would say, 'that's where everyone goes,' as if this fact were enough to discredit the destination. 'I was doing some research online,' he would say, basically telling her that he was planning on ruining what she had hoped was going to be a relaxing and uneventful trip, 'and apparently there's this beach. . . .' So instead of going to the famous place that everyone they knew had been to, they would go on an unpredictable quest in search of a hidden gem that was supposedly better than anything the more popular spots had to offer. But all of this wouldn't have bothered her if it weren't for the fact that more often than not they never even ended up at this alleged paradise that hardly anyone else knew about, and even if they did manage to get there it was always a huge disappointment. They might spend the night walking along a deserted country road, no shoulder to protect them whenever a car drove by every couple of hours, so they'd jump down into the roadside ditch and then crawl back out once the car had passed. Maybe James had heard or read about a restaurant that was *extremely authentic*, the sort of place that tourists were always trying to get to but could never find, where the customs and food had been *preserved*. Unlike the tourist traps that they were constantly trying to avoid but invariably ended up visiting, these authentic restaurants and hotels did not offer themselves up. They refused to meet you halfway. Everything was on their terms. Instead of trying to make themselves understood and translating their customs into terms a tourist could understand, these authentic places carried on in the same way they always had, and it was up to you to figure it out. An authentic place didn't need tourists, in fact tourists eventually ruin authentic places, which is why James was so obsessed with these restaurants and hotels, or beaches and lookouts – they hadn't been ruined yet, they were still unique and peculiar to their time and place, they hadn't been transformed into one of the placeless and timeless cultural voids that people refer to as tourist traps. He was so determined to find these authentic hideouts that he was willing to charge blindly into the most precarious and unfavourable circumstances. Up to her knees in ditchwater, Mary would break down and start screaming that she would never let him do this to her again. This was the last time his deranged infatuation with authenticity would lead them to an obscure Spanish town that nobody had heard of, not even the Spanish people they had spoken with in cafés and on buses as they passed through the equally obscure towns they had to go through to get there and to a cantina that James had read about in a travel magazine, where you could apparently watch one of the last great masters of Flamenco perform. What did it matter if she was the greatest living Flamenco dancer when they knew absolutely nothing about Flamenco and had never even seen it performed? Why couldn't they have stayed in the city and caught one of the dozen excellent dancers featured nightly? She just wanted to have a nice relaxing vacation but instead they were stranded on a stretch of country road, diving into the fucking ditch every time one of these maniacs flew by, the only sign of life being the sounds of howling dogs (especially frightening because they hadn't seen a house for miles). So when they finally came across a house with a light on, she forced James to knock on the door and ask if they could use their phone to call a cab. But the man that came to the door was clearly confused and James couldn't make himself understood, so after a flurry of pointing and nodding and saying 'si, si' about a thousand times they found themselves sitting in the back of the man's truck as he drove them to the bus station that they had set out from about four hours before. This was how James's little quests usually turned out. They would reach some sort of crisis and he would admit that he wasn't sure they were headed the right way so they ended up giving up on reaching the authentic restaurant, or waterfall, or whatever, and on their way back Mary would point out that they could have just gone to the inauthentic tourist trap where they wouldn't even have noticed how inauthentic it actually was, and they may have even had a good time. Because, in her experience, when James actually did pull it off and locate one of these authentic places, they ended up being run-down (if it was a restaurant or hotel) or underwhelming (if it was a beach or waterfall) and she couldn't help thinking that the reason that the other places, the ones they avoided, were so popular and overrun with tourists was because they were better. Sitting and listening to James drag out the story of his encounter with the sketchy drug addict, she is suddenly overcome by the same sinking feeling she gets once she realizes that James has tricked her into one of his stupid quests for authenticity. She no longer has the patience to listen to him talk about whether he ended up handing over the four hundred dollars (as though there was ever any question). 'The definition of insanity,' her dad used to say, 'is to do the same thing over and over again and expect a different result.' This annoying maxim, which her dad would trot out whenever he stood over Mary and watched as she tried and failed at a task he was eager to demonstrate, and which she's since discovered is ridiculously common, precisely described James's behaviour. Here he is telling her about getting tricked by a maniac as though it was completely unheard of, when in actual fact it happened all the time. James doesn't say, 'I did it again.' He says, 'I can't believe what I just did.' He doesn't come right out and tell her that he gave away more of their money to a good-looking street person, even though he does this so often that the reason he is so nervous and is dragging out the story for so long is because he wants to convince her that *this time it was different.* 'Why the fuck would you believe some horseshit story about a fucking money order?' she asks, interrupting him before he's actually admitted to giving the stranger the money. 'That's my point,' he says, 'I didn't believe him. I knew the whole thing was a scam. He wouldn't even let me see the form. And just the way he was acting was a dead giveaway, he was all shifty and either he wouldn't look me in the eyes, or he stared at me so intensely I thought he was going to confess to a murder or something like that.' 'So I don't understand then,' she says, 'if it was so obvious that the guy was a *junkie,* why the fuck did you give him the money?' James looks a bit surprised, 'How do you know I gave him the money?' he asks.

'Because it's fucking obvious,' she screams. He signals frantically for her to keep her voice down. 'Jesus,' he says, 'you'll wake the fucking neighbours.' 'I don't care about the fucking neighbours,' she continues to scream. 'What is wrong with you? Seriously? It's distressing. I know you're not an idiot. You're actually pretty smart. So what is it then? Are you crazy? Is that it? Are you crazy and just really good at hiding it?' She is no longer sitting, and has been pacing the floor in front of the couch, waving her arms in the air like a cartoon depiction of a hysterical wife. James is cowering on the corner of the couch and when Mary pauses to catch her breath he speaks up, 'You're not understanding me,' he explains, 'I know that giving four hundred dollars to a stranger is completely insane. I'm not crazy. That's what I've been trying to explain to you, if you'd just let me finish.' James is more than a little hurt that Mary expects the worst from him, and that she assumed he gave the stranger four hundred dollars (even though this is *technically* what happened). He begins to despair. It isn't that he can't understand why Mary would be angry that he'd once again done something seemingly naive and detrimental to their finances, but he thought she still believed in him enough to listen to his reason for doing something so stupid and maybe even insane. He'd been certain, as he made his way home after the encounter with the con man, that if she would hear him out then he'd be able to make her understand why he gave away four hundred dollars in full knowledge that he was being scammed. But now that he is sitting on the couch as Mary paces the floor in front of him, screaming at him and waving her arms, he isn't even sure if his explanation makes any sense. What had been so reasonable, and even a little comical, now struck him as nonsense, so after begging for her to hear him out he found himself at a loss for what to say next. 'What could you possibly say,' Mary seethes, 'that would explain why you would give someone four hundred dollars except that you're a fucking idiot? Seriously,' she stops in front of him and glares, 'what sort of twisted logic are you going to use to try to convince me that somehow this wasn't your fault? Unless you're going to tell me that I'm wrong and you didn't give this guy four hundred dollars, or that you're lying about the whole thing as some kind of sick fucking joke. Aside from that there's nothing you can say that will convince me that you're not fucking crazy.' James stands up to face her, 'What the fuck are you talking about?' he screams. 'Crazy? Are you serious? How can you even say that? You won't even listen to me and now you've decided that I'm crazy? This is fucking ridiculous,' he storms into the hallway as if he's going to leave, and then turns around and starts shouting at her as she stands at the other end. 'Why is it that I must be crazy?' he roars, as if addressing a large outdoor crowd and not his wife, in the confines of their apartment. 'Why is that the only possible reason for giving someone four hundred dollars?' 'Because you do this sort of shit all the fucking time,' Mary shrieks. 'That's the textbook definition of crazy. You do the same thing all the time and even though a fucking child could tell you what's going to happen you seem to think that things are going to turn out differently.' James is painfully aware that their neighbours can hear them through the thin walls of their apartment, so he softens his voice in an attempt to calm things down. He made a mistake by getting angry, but if he could get things back to a calmer state he is confident he can turn things around. This may have even worked if he'd said something to placate Mary to show that he was sorry for giving away their hard-earned money to a complete stranger, instead of what he actually said, which ends up making everything a whole lot worse. 'Listen,' he says, 'I get why you're upset and I can understand why you would think that giving four hundred dollars to someone that I was more or less certain was a con artist is something only a crazy person would do, and what I'm about to say may sound even crazier, but the reason I gave that guy four hundred dollars was because I wanted to believe that he was telling me the truth, even though I knew he wasn't. I *wanted* to be wrong. I know it doesn't make a lot of sense but I don't think what I did was crazy, I think it was sort of an act of faith, or something. Do you know what I mean?' This isn't what he'd planned on saying, at least not in these words, but now that he'd said it he finds it has the ring of truth, and he elaborates on it as if he's been contemplating the thought for a long time. James believes he's being completely honest, and that on account of his honesty, Mary couldn't help but understand why he did what he did, even though he didn't really understand it himself. 'Why would I say something so ridiculous,' he says, 'and that reflects so poorly on my sense of judgment, unless I was desperate for you to understand that I hadn't been conned, at least not in the way you think, but that I gave him the four hundred dollars because I wanted to?' These words, instead of building something up, turn out to have an annihilating effect. Mary sits on the couch absolutely destroyed by what James has just said, and for a brief moment she stares blankly ahead, until she's finally overcome and slumps into the cushions. Her change is so sudden that it takes James a second to realize that she isn't laughing but is in fact crying. It is a wild, despairing sort of crying. Just a couple of seconds before, she'd been consumed with anger and disgust for what James had done, but his words have annihilated these emotions so that all that is left is howling despair. She knows that she doesn't have real cause for despair, on the surface of her life things are relatively trouble-free, and she feels guilty for giving in to these feelings of helplessness. Somehow, though, despite all they had going for them, she is now convinced that she is trapped in the most hopeless and meaningless life that a person could ever have the misfortune of getting stuck with. She wails and sobs, the full extent of her despair seizing her with singular ferocity. James sits next to her and puts his arm around her shoulders and she doesn't even bother to shake him off. His touch doesn't soothe her. Far from comforting, it only serves to increase her loneliness. Here she is, plunged into the deepest despair, and the very same person who used to be able to reassure her is now the primary cause of her insecurity, and every attempt he makes to take on his former role reveals how irrevocable the situation really is. How did this happen? What had they done wrong? Why did even the most basic contact seem hopelessly out of reach? James pulls her closer and she doesn't pull away, but neither does she give in to him. She just sits there sobbing and wailing, letting him awkwardly wrap his arms around her because even though his attempt to console her only makes her feel worse, there's something liberating about letting this feeling take hold. It feels as though something has come undone, or that they have finally gone too far or waited too long and whatever they'd been waiting on had already passed by or would never come. She feels desperate to have it all out, to face up to everything they missed from not paying attention or from looking the other way, focussing on the minor scenes from life without realizing that it's all part of one long movie that's been playing on a loop. But even as she struggles to comprehend the entirety of their failure, she knows that it is impossible to keep the whole thing in her head. Life together is too complex. Maybe in some earlier era, when life was slower and things came one at a time, instead of all at once, it was possible to see the whole thing in a glance, to have it before your eyes while you were busy milking the cows or whatever. But now it is as though this lifelong movie isn't only about her own little world, but all the other worlds in existence, and those that existed long ago and only flicker across the screen for a second, as though the movie she is watching has been running since the beginning of time, as though the loop is getting bigger and bigger, and it was only possible to have a dim sense of how they might plausibly fit into the bigger picture. In short, it feels like they were born too late. That it

was no longer possible to know what roles they were supposed to play because all the roles have been taken. Even if
Mary had been born twenty years earlier she's pretty sure
she would've been better off. Everybody she knows feels the
same way. 'We all feel like the party is over,' she thinks, 'like
we showed up just as everyone else was leaving.' All the
good times have already been had and the most that they
can hope for is to keep the memories of those days alive.
That's how Mary and her friends deal with their crushing
nostalgia, by staging tiny recreations of things they never
really experienced. Her friend Anna spends her life avoiding mass-produced food, growing her own vegetables, and
even going so far as slaughtering the animals that she eats.
Then there's Damion, who refuses to watch movies made
after 1951. But these are just extreme examples of what is a
general and pervasive affliction. We're convinced that life
used to be better, simpler. We go for a drive and all we can
think about is how much better it must've been when the
cars were slower and the roads were narrower and nobody
was in a hurry, or at least not the white-knuckled frenzy
that we drive in now. Time keeps adding up. We can't get
on top of it. Mary's friends with children are overwhelmed
by the enormity of what they have to face. Autism, juvenile
depression, stone fruit allergies, social anxiety, sexting, the
private school system versus the public school system, au-
tomatic weapons, gluten, global capitalism. It's impossible
to anticipate every disaster that life has to offer and the in-
evitability of their failure as parents forces them into a de-
fensive crouch, huddling over their children and swatting

away everything that comes near them. If only they lived in a time when their children could go out alone without the threat of being abducted. A nauseous feeling comes over Mary. She lets up on crying for a moment because this nausea is overwhelming. The memory of the cat – the way it hung its head when she started walking towards it, that sucking sound getting louder because of its terror over what she was going to do – every movement, each sound, were clearly signs of an animal in severe pain and distress, but Mary immediately thought she was the one in danger, so she saw everything the cat did as a threat. 'Maybe this is what I do with James?' she thinks. 'And because I'm so afraid I end up ignoring what is staring me right in the face. Maybe the cat is a sign.' James senses that something is happening and throws his other arm around her and pulls her into a hug, as if he is trying to smother her train of thought, or trying to distract her with intimacy. But now she pushes him off and slides into the far corner of the couch. She is like a TV detective, not the new kind that wallows in blood and semen and stares into the abyss of human perversity with the hard gaze of the chosen few who have enough courage and genius to see the world for what it is, but more like the older ones, who sometimes seemed to know everything but at other times were just as confused as everyone else, and more often than not were only a few steps ahead of us so we could flatter ourselves by thinking we would've come to the same conclusion even if they hadn't been leading us on, and, just like these old-fashioned TV detectives, Mary feels she is on the verge of some revelation, and if she can keep her mind still for just a second then everything will fall into place. James tries to catch her eye to get an idea of what she could possibly be thinking, but she stares straight ahead with a blank expression. She's trying to exclude everything from her thoughts, when all at once, after James puts his hand on her arm, it's there before her, so clear and real that she feels like she could take a picture of it. 'Neither of us believe in what we're doing,' she says, and finally she turns to look at James. 'What?' he says. 'What do you mean? What are you saying?' She smiles as if she wants to reassure him, the way a kindly civil servant might if they were dealing with someone desperate and foreign who couldn't speak the language but clearly needed help, which in all likelihood the civil servant wouldn't be able to provide. She doesn't want James to worry, even though she is now thinking that she might leave him. 'We don't have any faith in what we're doing,' she says. 'It's like we don't know what else to do, so we keep doing the same thing over and over again without believing that anything is ever going to happen.' 'Are you talking about getting pregnant?' James asks. 'I'm talking about everything,' she says. James stands up and for an instant it looks as if he might give in to a terrible rage, but then he slumps back into the couch, deciding that it isn't worth it, seeing in Mary's face that it didn't matter how loud he screamed or whether he started punching walls or throwing things around the room. She can see now what the truth had been all along. It's useless to try to get her to see it in some other way. He hangs his head between his legs and says nothing and waits as if he's been found out by the aforementioned TV detective. And without even noticing that he'd started, he's now sobbing just as uncontrollably as Mary had been only moments earlier. Seeing him fall apart in a matter of seconds takes Mary out of the stupor of her own revelation and she looks over at him as if she's only just realized who he is, where they are, and what is happening. The doorbell rings as she's sliding across the couch to comfort James. They both freeze. And then, without a word or signal of any kind, they both make for the basement steps at the same time. James eases the door open silently and they creep down the stairs as if they were *intruders in their own home,* feeling their way through the darkness to the ratty couch. James carefully gathers the papers and books piled on the cushions and soundlessly places them in neat stacks on the floor. Mary waits wordlessly for him to finish and then they lie down together in the spoon position. The faint sound of the doorbell drifts around upstairs, followed by the dull thudding of someone's fist against the door. James runs his fingers over the waistband of her pyjama bottoms and Mary pushes her ass into his crotch. He pulls her shirt up and squeezes her breasts with his free hand as she squirms against him. Her shirt is up around her neck and his arm is pinned under her shoulders so it juts out awkwardly, and she's reached back behind her to clumsily rub him over his jeans. They suddenly get fed up with this position. James jerks his arm out from under Mary, raises himself on his elbow so he can get his cock out while Mary turns face down and tugs her pants to her knees. Then he straddles her legs and she reaches back and spreads her ass cheeks, but he can't manage it with his jeans still on, so he rolls on his side and pulls them off. 'Hurry up,' she hisses. Someone is still ringing the doorbell. He gets back on top of her but with her legs pressed together he's having a hard time pushing into her. 'Just go,' she moans, and with that he forces himself all the way into her cunt. He braces his arms on either side of her and they have at it like that, in a total frenzy. 'I'm going to come,' he says, and when he rolls off of her she starts to laugh. 'What is it,' he whispers, but she's laughing hysterically and doesn't answer. He starts laughing along with her, occasionally uttering 'What?' and then waiting before asking again, 'What is it?' When she finally calms down she rolls over to face him and, even though there are no lights on, the little window right above them lets in enough streetlight for him to see that her face is covered in tears. 'I came at the same time,' she says. He falls back on the couch and starts laughing again, now just as hysterically as Mary had been. 'Just like in the movies,' she blurts out before she starts laughing again. 'It must be a sign,' he manages to get out between fits of giggling. 'Exactly,' she says, 'it means we're meant to be together.' They both roar at this for a while before settling back down so they're lying on their sides, facing each other and smiling. The doorbell sounds out above them. 'That must be the neighbours about their cat,' she says. 'Or maybe it's the stranger,' he whispers. She smiles, assuming he's trying to be funny. 'I almost wish it was.' They both stare at the basement stairs. 'Well,' she says, 'we should probably go tell them what happened.'

GIVING UP

About the Author

Mike Steeves lives with his wife and child in Montreal. *Giving Up* is his first novel.

Colophon

Distributed in Canada by the Literary Press Group:
www.lpg.ca

Distributed in the United States by Small Press
Distribution: www.spdbooks.org

Shop online at www.bookthug.ca

BOOK
PRODUCTION
WAR ECONOMY
STANDARD

Edited for the press by Malcolm Sutton
Copy edited by Ruth Zuchter
Designed by Malcolm Sutton
Typeset in Portrait Text